MISTLETOE MADNESS

DARCI BALOGH

Knowhere Media LLC

Copyright © 2018 by Darci Balogh
All rights reserved.
ISBN: 978-1-943990-32-0

No part of this book may be reproduced or transmitted in any form or by any means, electronic or mechanical, including photocopying, recording or my any information or storage and retrieval systems without written permission from the author and publisher.

The characters and events portrayed in this book are fictitious. Any similarity to real persons, living or dead, is coincidental and not intended by the author.

Unattributed quotations are by Darci Balogh.

Cover design by GetCovers

For my sister, Robin.

Thank you for your enthusiasm for life, for projects, for building forts, and especially your enthusiasm for Christmas.

Your spirit has always been an inspiration to me and your skill at creating an ambience and a sense of fun wherever you go and whatever the circumstances is nothing short of miraculous. I love Christmas, and you are a big reason why. May we share countless more holidays and every days together, and may your Christmas always be merry and bright!

Chapter One

Abigail spent the first day in tears. The second day she wallowed in self-pity and frustration. The third, fourth, fifth, and sixth day she toiled away, desperately searching for freelance gigs online. And on the seventh day, December 1st, Abigail started packing up her apartment.

Getting fired had come as a shock. Getting fired immediately after Thanksgiving had ended a year that started off tentatively bad and was wrapping up bang on horrible.

She began the year with a break up from her on-again, off-again, never committing boyfriend. If you could really call him that.

Then she'd been demoted to part-time in her position as a contract graphic designer for a mid-level, sometimes sleazy, marketing firm.

In the middle of the summer her unofficial roommate had moved out to get married to an attractive and successful engineer she'd met online. Leaving Abigail to shoulder rent and utility payments by herself on her part-time salary.

In an attempt to do something positive, Abigail had

planned a two week trip home to see her parents and brother for the Christmas season. Graphic design work was notoriously slow around that time of year. Companies were usually focusing on getting through the holidays before they started big new projects at the beginning of the year. But when she brought up her upcoming time off during a video meeting the weekend after Thanksgiving break, her supervisor, Jennifer, surprised her with an out of the blue announcement.

"Actually, Abby, I have some unfortunate news."

Abigail hated to be called 'Abby', but nobody at this virtual job had ever gotten that memo.

"Oh, what's the news?" Abigail asked, blissfully ignorant for a few more moments that her life was about to be completely dismantled.

"I'm sorry to have to tell you this, but we don't need your services anymore," Jennifer's two dimensional face said, looking at Abigail with a mixture of authority and sympathy from the computer screen.

A few beats went by as Abigail's brain processed the information. Then her mouth dropped open and her already long and thin nose pinched together at the top with what could only be described as an expression of anguish. Blotches of red climbed from her pale neck to her pale cheeks. She looked like one of the angry birds from that game, the red one, except with an out of control curly mop of dark hair that bordered on frizzy. Her mouth opened and closed several times as she tried to think of a response, giving her the appearance of a dying, blotchy, outraged fish.

Abigail knew without doubt that's what she looked like, because she could see her face in the small square at the bottom right of her computer screen. Courtesy of Zoom.

"I'm sorry to be the bearer of bad news," Jennifer said, alarmed at Abigail's reaction. "The company is moving in a different direction and we just can't justify the expense of another graphic designer."

In retrospect, Abigail wished she'd had the wherewithal to click her computer camera to the off position. That would at least have prevented Jennifer from watching her cry.

"Abby?" Jennifer's natural style and grace was having a hard time not reacting to Abigail's crumpled, tragic image, which was full screen on her end, Abigail remembered later with much embarrassment. "Are you all right?"

"No," Abigail managed. "I'm not!"

That's when she dropped her face into her hands and wept, rather uncontrollably. She tried to stop crying so she could leave with at least a shred of dignity, or at least give Jennifer a piece of her mind with some scathing exit commentary.

Neither of those things happened, however. Abigail just kept bawling into her hands, her face getting redder and her nose filling with snot until she reached out blindly and found the mouse on her desk. Abigail glanced up briefly to make sure she clicked on the End Call button. She saw Jennifer's shocked and uncomfortable face for one horrible moment before it disappeared from her computer monitor forever.

She was out. Fired. Done.

The humiliation turned to fear turned to shock turned to anger, then back to humiliation, and the whole process started again.

She'd never been fired before. It was not something she knew how to deal with or something she was prepared to handle. Emotionally or financially.

Her meager savings had burned up covering full rent since her roommate left. She'd been considering asking her parents for a small loan to help out until she could either pick up more work or find a new roommate. That wasn't the main reason she was going home for the holiday, but it had been on her mind.

She couldn't ask them to cover her expenses completely, though. That was too much. She was a grown woman, after all. Fully capable of paying her own way in life, usually.

Then there was the unfortunate timing of her lease ending on December 5th. There was no way her dusty old landlord was going to renew a lease with her if she didn't have a job. He wasn't that kind of landlord. The nice kind. He'd never liked her much, anyway, but he was fastidious about doing a full review of all tenant's financial circumstances before signing any paperwork. Even tenants who had lived there for six years.

For several days following her virtual dismissal Abigail experienced bouts of anger. She would rail at the empty room around her the way she wished she would have railed at Jennifer when she let her go, or Tom when they broke up. She found that it didn't matter how recent the wrong, she was angry at anyone and everyone who she harbored any resentment towards. Nobody was immune from becoming the unknowing victim of her verbal outrage.

"Moving in a new direction? Could that new direction possibly be overseas where you can hire a graphic designer for $5 an hour instead of $30? Would that be the direction this company is moving, Jennifer?" Abigail practically shouted at her kitchen cupboards as she was looking for potato chips or cookies or any kind of junk food she could use to assuage her disappointment.

Then, when she ran out of groceries, "Can't take time off work to go out, Tom? Really? I saw you out two nights ago on Instagram. Who was that red head you were with, Tom? Would it really be that difficult to call or text and invite me to go with you? And on that note, when was the last time you called or texted me first? When, Tom?" Abigail whispered intensely to herself as she walked through the grocery store buying Ramen soup and eggs to get by for the next few days on next to no cash.

Being a contract worker meant she billed on Saturday for all of the work she'd done that week and was paid the following Wednesday. With Thanksgiving being a slow week, Abigail barely had enough money in her last paycheck to pay for gas to drive to her parent's house, let alone groceries.

In retrospect, it really had been a horrible job. No benefits, no vacation or sick time, high expectations for less and less billable hours. She wasn't even sure she liked doing graphic design anymore. Dealing with clients was always stressful and often infuriating.

"Honey, why don't you just come home for Christmas and stay with us for a while?" Her Mom had asked when Abigail called with the news.

"I don't want to impose," she answered miserably.

"What, impose?" Her Mother scoffed at the idea, "Zeke only moved out three years ago. Do you think him living here all that time was an imposition?"

Yes, that's exactly what Abigail thought, but she didn't dare say it to her mother.

"What's going on?" She heard her father's distant voice over the phone. He was asking her mother to explain their conversation. When she called her parent's house, she never only spoke to one of them. They conversed as a team.

"It's Abigail, she's coming home to live with us for a while," her mother explained to her father, her voice a little dimmer because she had loosely covered the mouthpiece with her hand.

"Leaving the big city?" he asked, surprised.

"She lost her job," her mother's voice had become a hissing whisper, yet Abigail could still make out every word.

"Oh, that's a shame," her Dad answered. "Tell her to come on home. Zeke's apartment is empty."

Zeke was short for Ezekiel, her older brother by just one year. Zeke had dropped out of college midway and ended up living back at home until he figured out what he wanted to do when he grew up, which was apparently own a used book store.

Three years ago he bought a run down old building in the run down old part of their home town and opened a used book store and coffee shop called The Thinking Bean. Then he moved into the tiny upstairs apartment above this fine establishment and left his basement apartment their parents had remodeled for him empty.

"Did you hear that, honey?" her Mom asked. "Come home. Zeke's apartment is empty."

"Yes, I heard," Abigail answered. Despite her best efforts, she could tell she was going to cry.

※

LEAVING MOST of her furniture behind wasn't too difficult. Much of it had been thrift store purchases or left behind by her roommate who'd moved on to a posher existence when she married her engineer.

Abigail packed only her most precious possessions, which included many, many books, into her modest hatchback. Once she included her dishes, her clothes, her bedding, a couple plants she'd managed to keep alive over the years, her computer, and the few pieces of artwork that she actually liked, her car was loaded top to bottom. She couldn't even see out of her rear view mirror.

As torn up as she'd been about losing her job and not being able to find a new one fast enough to stay in her apartment, she had to admit she felt a little relieved when she pulled out of her assigned parking space and dropped the keys into the landlord's mailbox. She couldn't comfortably afford this place by herself, even at a full time salary. And she'd learned a few things.

She'd learned that she wasn't really cut out for roommates. She was a loner. She also knew that she needed to find a better job, a company job maybe, someplace that would value her creativity and pay her accordingly.

Abigail pulled onto the highway and headed southwest. It would take her 17 hours to drive to Pitkin Point, home of her family and all of her teenage angst. A place she swore she would never return to live unless she could build the biggest house in town and ride around in a limousine all day. This wasn't quite the homecoming she'd fantasized about. Without enough money to even spend on a hotel to break up the drive, she was planning on stopping occasionally in busy parking lots and napping in her car if she got tired. Asking her parents for help with money right now seemed like too much. They were already going to put her up.

She had that much to be thankful for and she refused to worry over the dissatisfaction and unpopularity of her youth. So she wasn't coming home as some rich man's wife or a famous artist or movie star. She was lucky to have a welcoming place to go in order to regroup and get her life in order. There was no way it was going to take longer than a few months before she was gone again. She could handle that.

Realizing that she'd forgotten her phone in the bottom of her purse, which was nestled safe and completely out of reach behind her seat, she turned on the radio. Christmas music.

She'd all but forgotten about Christmas after everything she'd just went through. A new wave of irritation rippled through her at the cold and inconsiderate way she'd been let go right before Christmas. Was she really surprised? That place had never treated her with much respect, they used her and threw her away on a whim, without ever truly offering her anything substantial.

Suddenly, Tom's face flashed through her mind. Abigail had to chuckle at a realization that came to her just as she was passing the highway sign telling her it was 46 miles to Springfield.

The parallels between her ex-boyfriend, Tom, and the horrible job she'd just lost were eerie. Each of them kept her around just enough to restrict her ability to look for something better, in boyfriends and in jobs. She remained in a continual holding pattern around both of them, waiting, watching, and never allowed to either land and be safe on the ground or fly away to greener pastures.

"Good riddance," Abigail said out loud.

She decided right there and then that this would mark a new moment in her life, one free of settling for anything less than what she truly wanted and deserved. In work or in love.

Happy with her decision, she turned up the radio. 'Jingle Bell Rock' was playing and Abigail sang along, only 16 hours and 40 minutes left until she was home for Christmas.

Chapter Two

Driving through Pitkin Point at 2:00 am was like driving through a ghost town. Nobody, absolutely nobody, was awake. There were no lights on anywhere, except the street lamps, which were thick on Main Street, but grew sparse in the residential areas.

Abigail weaved the hatchback down the short quaint streets of her childhood, taking in some of the differences that stood out against her memories.

Some of the familiar houses had changed their faces with different color schemes, new landscaping or remodeling. The Schmidts had built a new garage next to their house. The Petersons had added a second story. All of the trees were much bigger, while the houses all looked smaller. Maybe they appeared so because of the growth of the trees, or maybe it was because Abigail viewed them through her grown up eyes. It was difficult to say.

She automatically turned down the music in her car as she approached her parent's home and pulled slowly and quietly into the driveway, if it was possible to actually drive quietly. The brick ranch home was the only one on the street with lights still spilling from its windows. Abigail knew it was unlikely her parents had stayed up this late, but they were welcoming her home with light. Abigail smiled at the idea that they had left lamps on in order to make it easier for her to find her way around when she could easily walk through this house blindfolded.

They had also left the Christmas lights on in the front yard. She assumed other houses in the neighborhoods had decorated their yards as well, but turned them off when they went to sleep for the night.

Not her parents.

Her parents were a little over the top with their yard ornamentation. They collected outdoor Christmas decorations and their display had grown over the years.

Her father was Jewish, although he didn't practice the religion of his youth. He had always embraced the Christian holidays to make his wife happy, but his tastes in Christmas decorations leaned towards the secular. As did her mother's, who was not the type to attach to a particular religion or church. For that reason their yard was full of Christmas polar bears, penguins, dogs, cats, one large moose, a tiny llama, and a whole herd of deer.

The wire framed animals made of tiny white or colored lights were grouped together geographically, making it look like the herd of deer were migrating across the front of the lawn towards the driveway, the penguins were tightly packed together for warmth in the corner flower bed, the polar bears were lurking in the shrubs waiting to pounce on the penguins, the moose lumbered along the lilac bushes, the llama was up on a raised bed as if on the side of a mountain, and the dogs and cats were all near the front steps waiting to be let into the house. Abigail's gaze drifted over the bright and happy, if a little goofy, scene. It was good to be home.

She stepped out of the car, grabbed her purse and

overnight bag, and went to the front door. She tried the doorknob and found it unlocked, not surprising. Pitkin Point was very small. Everyone knew everyone else. This made it a safe place to live, although Abigail, after living in the city, had convinced her parents to at least lock their doors when they went to bed at night. They agreed and to her knowledge kept up that practice, except tonight. Tonight they were expecting her to arrive late.

When she stepped into the well lit entryway the smells of home hit her first.

What did home smell like, exactly? Abigail didn't really know. Maybe it was her mother's cooking, or the lemon spray she used when she dusted the wood, or her father's wool hat and coat hanging on the coat rack right behind the door. She couldn't say for certain. The combination of all of the scents in the house created the singular smell that made her feel safe and loved. She took in a deep breath.

"Sweetie," her father's voice, deep and sleepy, came from the adjoining living room. Abigail jumped a little, startled to find anyone awake.

"Dad?"

By habit, she peeked around the partial wall towards his reclining chair. She could just see his legs stuck out on the extended leg rest, his feet wiggling inside thick black socks.

"I wanted to make sure you got in," he mumbled a little as he put the recliner into sitting position and stood up. His glasses and the book he'd been reading slid off of his lap and landed softly on the carpet by his feet.

"You didn't have to wait up for me." She made her way to his chair and gave him a warm hug.

"Your mother was worried about you driving all that way," he said into her hair.

"It wasn't bad."

Abigail stooped down and picked up his glasses and book

while her Dad, Marty Ackerman, rubbed the sleep out of his eyes. He was a tall man, slumped now a little with age, but still broad and masculine, with a large nose to match his other strong facial features, and kind brown eyes. His hair was almost completely grey, but still thick and unruly, with a few remnants of the deep black it once had been.

"Thank you," he said as she gave him his items and kissed him on the cheek. Fully awake now he slipped on his glasses and gazed at her face carefully. Then he put his large hand on the side of her head and stroked her hair. "It's good to see you, sweetie." He leaned down so he could reach her forehead, and kissed it.

"You, too, Dad," she smiled.

"You tired?" he asked. She nodded. "Come on, your mother fixed up Zeke's old room for you. It's a lot more...feminine than it was." He moved towards the stairway that led to the basement, picking up her overnight bag she'd left in the entryway as he did.

❋

WAKING up the next morning in Zeke's room instead of the room she had grown up in was both familiar and disorienting. Her old bedroom, located next to her parent's room on the main floor, had long ago been converted to a sewing room for her mother. Zeke's basement bedroom was a little bit bigger than hers, had but one full sized window, which, though it let in light, still only offered a view of the window well.

There was a new quilt on the dark wood four poster bed and a matching valance on the window. The quilt was in a flower pattern, using dark greens, light greens, white and a wide range of different shades of pink and red swatches. This, Abigail assumed, was her mother's feminization of Zeke's old space. Her Mom was a self proclaimed textile artist and quilting was her passion. Abigail liked this one, the pattern and colors almost made it look like a field of poppies.

Her eyes had fluttered open just as the morning light made its first attempts to penetrate the window well. The plants she and her Dad had brought in from her car the night before to prevent from freezing sat neatly on a white bookshelf just under the window. As Abigail rolled onto her back and stretched, she noticed that the walls were bare and was glad she would have a place to hang her artwork. Sometimes her mother decorated to the point nothing could be added without going into sensory overload, but she hadn't done that this time.

She was up early. Her body clock was still running on Eastern time, which meant she was two hours ahead of everyone else here. Her Dad had waited up late, plus her Mom was never one to get up too early in the morning. It would be a while before they were awake.

Abigail had a thought to do something nice and go pick up pastries for breakfast. She had a few dollars left in her bank account, she could splurge on her parents.

Plus, it would give her a chance to drop by Zeke's and wake him up early. She hadn't seen her brother in over two years. It would be fun to bug him a little bit and get a look at his new digs, now that she was taking over his old ones.

Driving through the freezing, empty streets of Pitkin Point at dawn was almost as desolate as driving through them at 2:00 am. There were a few more people up and around, a handful of cars rolled down the streets. The two stop lights on Main, however, were still set to blinking red and would stay that way until 7:00 am when the town officially woke up.

At this hour of the day, two places were open; the gas station and the bakery. The latter was owned and operated by John and Judy Halina.

Judy was probably what everyone in Pitkin Point considered Abigail's closest childhood friend. Abigail would agree with that statement, although 'closest friend' was a relative concept. Still, as she pulled into one of the several empty parking spaces in front of the bakery, Take the Cake, Abigail was both nervous and excited to see Judy.

"Well look what the cat drug in," Judy exclaimed from behind an orange and cream striped counter that almost completely hid her from view. Judy was a tiny woman. She'd been so small as a child that, if she folded her legs together properly, she could fit comfortably inside Abigail's backpack with just her head sticking out of the top. Taller now, but only just, Judy had gorgeous smooth skin and shining black hair that hung down to her hips. Her natural beauty was only slightly diminished by the ridiculous orange and cream striped paper hat and matching apron she wore.

"Hi, Judy, got any doughnuts?" Abigail tried this as a lighthearted greeting and it seemed to work. Judy hurried around the counter and gave her a hug, asking what she was doing here and if she had time for a cup of coffee. "Not today," Abigail answered. "But I am here until after Christmas. We should get together," she added, and she meant it, even if her introverted habits balked at this kind of socializing. She left out the part of being jobless and homeless at the moment. That information would be readily available to everyone in town soon enough.

"Sure, absolutely," Judy responded, beaming at Abigail with small, perfect teeth. "Where are you off to this morning?"

"I'm going to wake Zeke up and surprise him," Abigail didn't have to say much about Zeke to Judy. She had often been a victim of his obnoxious big brother pranks when they hung out as kids.

"Oh, Zeke," Judy rolled her eyes jokingly. "He's practically certifiable, you know that, don't you?"

"Oh, I know," Abigail answered.

Judy showed her their doughnut inventory and Abigail chose a dozen, taking half cake and half raised, all with chocolate frosting. With a promise to schedule a time for coffee as soon as possible, Abigail said her goodbyes and took her paper box of doughnuts into the biting cold, anxious to get to Zeke's.

The building Zeke had purchased for the site of his brilliant used book store career was not too far from Take the Cake, but might as well have been a world away. Main Street gave way to Central, a quick right onto 2nd, follow 2nd for three blocks and there it was. Teetering on the corner of 2nd and Cherry stood the two story brick building that housed The Thinking Bean, the avant-garde used and rare bookstore combo coffee shop that nobody in this town ever wanted, or at least never knew they wanted.

The building was on the far end of a row of connected industrial type buildings built in the late 1800's. Most of these buildings had been out of use as far back as she could remember. Although she recalled one of them used to be some kind of storage place for animal feed or something of that nature.

If Pitkin Point had a bad area of town, this was it. Empty and abandoned, it reminded Abigail of some of the trendier places near her apartment—old apartment—where funky casual people sat on rickety wooden chairs and sucked down expensive drinks. All of those places had been forged out of similar unused old buildings like this one.

Balancing her doughnut box in one hand, Abigail took a chance on the front door and found it unlocked, big surprise. She shook her head, it was unbelievable that a business could leave their door open all night and not get robbed. Yet, here she was, wandering through The Thinking Bean looking for the stairway she knew was there somewhere that would lead her to the upstairs apartment while the owner slept.

The air inside the little bookstore was barely warmer than the low 20's outside. She wondered if Zeke kept it cold on purpose or if this was just an unfortunate aspect of an aged building.

"He probably keeps it this cold," she muttered to herself.

As she sought the stairs, Abigail took in all of the renovations Zeke had done. The entire first story of the building was floor to ceiling windows in the front. The windows were framed out in sections with black frames, giving them the look of an all glass garage door that could be opened up completely if desired.

The inside was split into two narrow sections that reached much farther back than expected. The first section, the one she entered through the front door, was the coffee shop section. The floor was painted concrete, the walls were exposed brick, and the ceiling had been painted in a black and white checkerboard pattern. There were eight tiny square tables with four bistro chairs each set up in the dining area. A used sofa, upholstered in plush dark red fabric, sat against one section of wall flanked by two equally used, and equally comfortable looking, reading chairs.

A polished wood counter provided a border to the coffee preparation area, which looked well equipped with a shining stainless steel commercial size espresso machine and open wooden shelves lined with white coffee cups of all shapes and sizes. An old fashioned looking cash register sat proudly on one end of the counter. Beside it was a large glass jar with a handwritten sign reading "Tips" taped to the side. There were a handful of bills and some change in the tip jar. Again, Abigail shook her head. It had been a long time since she'd been in such a trusting atmosphere.

An open doorway led from the coffee section of the shop

to the book section, which was equally long and narrow, but seemed even more so because every square inch of space of the walls were lined with books. Wood shelves, painted black, covered every wall from floor to ceiling and every shelf was stuffed with books. Handmade tags stuck out of the shelves at varying intervals with fat lettered writing that said things like "Fiction - Mystery - Aa" or "Non-fiction - Travel - Rr".

The narrow book section was separated into three sections by walls made of bookshelves which spanned the narrow space. A clever arched doorway led from section to section. Two fat chairs were shoved into the front up against the window, a modest end table on spindly legs between them.

Abigail was impressed despite her desire to be cynical. She ran her free hand along the spines of a line of paperbacks labeled, "Fiction - Fantasy, Dark - Ee", losing herself just a little bit in the presence of so many books.

She loved books. As did Zeke. Bookstores and libraries had always felt like places of refuge to her and her brother. An escape from the confusing demands of society. A place they could feel at home.

A heavy thump sounded upstairs, drawing her out of her thoughts. Excited to surprise her brother with doughnuts and, mostly, with her presence, Abigail located the cramped staircase at the back of the last section of books and made her way upstairs. At the top of the stairs was a small landing where she could look down over a banister and see the floor of the bookshop below.

She deduced that the one and only door on the opposite side of the landing must lead into Zeke's apartment. Hesitating for just a moment to wonder if she should knock first, she quickly decided 'no', and turned the knob, shoving the door open as fast as she could for effect.

The room was empty. Very anti-climactic.

"Hey, it's me," she shouted into the air. "Put some pants on, I brought breakfast."

Footsteps sounded from a dim hallway at the other end of the room. Abigail held the doughnuts up for display like she was on the Home Shopping Channel selling them to millions of viewers.

Zeke entered the room, a faded, dusty blue bath towel wrapped casually around his waist and another one flopped over his face as he rubbed it vigorously on his wet mop of hair. It appeared he had just gotten out of the shower.

"What?" A muffled voice came from under the towel.

Abigail's eyes widened as she instantly realized two shocking facts. First, this man was virtually naked. Second, this man was not her brother.

Chapter Three

Abigail stood frozen in place, her mouth hanging open in surprise, the doughnuts still poised at an attractive angle towards the stranger. A momentary irrational fear that if she moved, his towel might fall to the ground crossed her mind.

Without thinking, she looked the nearly naked body of the man in front of her up and down, taking in his wide shoulders, the muscles in them flexing as he rubbed his hair dry. He had a pleasingly muscular frame, not too pumped up like a body builder, but well formed and naturally masculine. A patch of dark chest hair, still damp from his shower, narrowed at the top of his abs, turning into a dark line that crept all the way down to his belly button and below, disappearing under the towel.

"What?" He said again, annoyance in his tone.

The stranger dropped his towel. The one that covered his head, thankfully, not the shabby blue one that hung loosely on his hips. Still, Abigail felt heat flash across her cheeks as her presence was revealed. She lifted the doughnut box higher, a feeble shield from his state of undress.

"Oh!" An involuntary yelp escaped her lips.

His eyes flew open, astonished at the sight of her. A few seconds passed when neither of them moved, not one muscle. Then surprise softened his shocked expression and turned it to recognition. He tilted his head an said, "Abby?"

Abigail was turned sideways, hiding behind the doughnut box and squinting as if looking at him through narrowed eyelids would reduce the amount of naked flesh she could see and make her intrusion a little less personal. She didn't notice the use of the despised nickname as much as she noticed the voice. She straightened up and stopped squinting.

"Jamie?"

His face transformed into a big, goofy smile. His wet, dark hair stuck out in all directions and he hadn't shaved yet, leaving him with a grown up manly stubble look than she'd ever seen on him before. But the sloped nose, the dopey grin, the way he was kind of bobbing his head up and down like a pigeon showing he was happy to see her, it was Jamie all right. No doubt about it.

"Abby, how are you?"

This time she heard the nickname and a wave of irritation came over her. What was Jamie Turner doing in Zeke's apartment?

Her gaze dropped to his towel, then lifted back to his face. Suddenly, Jamie remembered that he wasn't dressed. His shoulders hunched forward and he reached to secure the towel around his waist, accidentally loosening it in the process. Because of his bumbling, the towel slipped off his hips, dropping to his feet with a soft thud. The instant the towel slid out of reach, Jamie remembered he held a towel in his other hand. He quickly held that towel up against himself, saving her too much of a peep show.

"Jeez, Jamie!" Abigail exclaimed, squeezing her eyes shut

and holding the doughnut box directly in front of her face to add another visual blocker.

"Sorry, sorry," Jamie said.

She waited for his rustling to stop, then risked the slightest opening of one eye to see if he was decent. He was now safely wrapped, but still flustered.

"What are you doing here?" They asked each other at the same time.

Abigail scoffed, then opened her eyes just wide enough to glare at him as she demanded, "Where is Zeke?"

As if on cue, the sound of someone running up the stairs two at a time came to them. Jamie clenched the towel around his waist, checking that it was secure. Abigail knew him well enough to know that he wouldn't want Zeke to find him in a compromising position with her. She sniffed at him with thinly veiled distaste, then turned towards the door as her brother breezed into the room. His voice preceded him by a few moments, bellowing into the small apartment.

"Jamie, have you seen my sis–" Zeke stopped short when he saw her, his long face and wide mouth breaking into one of his amazing smiles. "Abbah Dabbah!" He opened his arms wide and wrapped her up into an infamous monkey hug. It took all of her concentration to keep hold of the doughnuts while he held her tight and rocked her side to side. "I saw your car out front," Zeke said, practically lifting her off the ground with the rocking.

Abigail wasn't short. She stood just under six feet tall, so it was unusual for her to feel dwarfed by anyone, even a man. However, Zeke was 6'6", and though he wasn't broad, his lean frame with its long, stretched limbs, was still formidable. She always felt small and dainty when she was with him. He pushed her away and held her at arm's length.

"You're squishing the doughnuts," she complained, not really upset.

"You look good for someone that just got fired," Zeke joked, his dark brown eyes laughing.

"You look hairy," she quipped. He did. He'd grown a substantial beard since she saw him last. His dark hair was thick and wavy, long enough to reach his ears, yet sticking out in all directions like he was a crazy professor who constantly ran his hands through his hair. "You look like a young Moses," she said, grinning at him.

"Very young," he answered, stroking his beard with one hand mimicking a wise old man. He finally noticed Jamie, who was still standing in his towel taking in the sibling reunion with a silly grin on his face. "Get some clothes on, man," Zeke commanded.

"Oh, right," Jamie snatched the escaped towel off the floor and retreated down the hallway.

Abigail leaned towards Zeke and whispered, "What is he doing here?"

"Jamie?" Zeke glanced at the hallway where Jamie had just disappeared, "He's crashing here for a while."

"Really?" Abigail scowled.

Zeke nudged her with his elbow. "He's single now, you know."

"Oh, God." Abigail made like she was gagging.

Zeke laughed his deep, contagious laugh, then added, "No, seriously, he got laid off a while ago. So he's staying here. He helps me fix up the place for cheap rent."

"Oh." Abigail still didn't like it. Jamie had been horrible to her when they were growing up. Always teasing, always playing stupid jokes. Her senior year she hadn't had a date to prom and he made fun of her for it, putting on an elaborate stunt just to embarrass her in front of her friends.

"What do you think?" Zeke asked.

"Well, I know you've always been friends, but he can be kind of a jerk," she told him.

Zeke look confused, then her words registered. "Jamie? Nah, he's all right," he dismissed her comment with a quick shake of his head. "I meant the place. What do you think of the place?"

She shrugged, not sure if she wanted to commit to an answer. Her reaction only encouraged Zeke. He grabbed her hand and drug her downstairs, giving her a tour of every inch of the bookshop and cafe area. She ended up sitting at one of the small cafe tables munching on a doughnut while Zeke prepared cappuccinos on the elaborate equipment behind the counter. About 7-ish, he went through his routine of opening the store.

First, he turned on all of the overhanging lights. Their warm glow lit up the corners of the room and brought out the texture of the exposed brick. The light made it possible to better see the paintings that hung along the walls by the tables. He'd told her that local artists brought their work to show and, hopefully, sell. She took her cappuccino as she got up to stand in front of the paintings, peering at each small, white tag with the name of the painting, name of the artist and price written in Zeke's scrawling hand.

"This is cool," she said, nodding towards the mini-art gallery.

"Yeah, I change them out every few months." He was at the thermostat, nudging the little red lever up to a higher temperature. "Sometimes we even sell one!" He added brightly.

"Why do you keep it so cold in here?" Abigail had not yet removed her coat and she held her cappuccino partly because she wanted to drink it, but also to keep her fingers warm.

"Because he's a Scrooge," Jamie answered her question. He'd slipped in when she wasn't looking and stood at the coffee machine behind the counter.

"Man up, Turner. Go get your blanky if you're cold," Zeke

called over his shoulder as he went to the front door and flipped the small open/closed sign over so the word 'Open' was facing out.

Jamie chuckled as he noisily prepared his drink. He was dressed, thank goodness, wearing jeans, tennis shoes and a long sleeve, olive green Henley shirt with the sleeves pushed up around his elbows. His hair was still damp, dark brown and not too short, but not as long as Zeke's. He had shaved and looked a little more like the Jamie she remembered, although not completely.

Since the last time she'd seen him, Jamie had grown into a man. He'd had that mid to late 20's growth spurt guys went through that took them from thin bodied and baby-faced into stronger, more angular, and hardened male specimens. As she watched him go through the elaborate motions necessary to fix a cappuccino, the long muscles in his forearms flexing, she had to admit that Jamie had grown into a pretty good looking man. Her mind wandered to the very recent memory of him in his towel, the dark trail of hair down the center of his stomach.

Jamie glanced her way and caught her staring. One side of his mouth lifted into a half-smile, almost a smirk. Abigail scowled and turned away, taking a sip of her drink, pretending she hadn't been looking at him at all.

"Maybe you'll paint something to put up?" Jamie suggested, carrying his drink to the table with the doughnut box and sitting down.

"Me?" She gave him a cursory glance over her shoulder before stepping further away to look at the next painting.

"Yeah, you," Jamie answered. "You still paint, don't you?"

Abigail didn't like having to talk with Jamie. She felt on edge, waiting for him to be sarcastic, "A little, I guess."

"You were always good," Jamie said before taking a sip of his drink.

Like he would know. Abigail rolled her eyes at the brick wall. Jerk.

"No, no, no, no, no!" Zeke took her by the arm and led her back to the table. "No time for making art. I've got bigger plans."

"Here we go." Jamie shook his head and took another sip.

Zeke sat her down next to Jamie before taking the chair on the other side. "I need your full attention and focus for something else, something bigger!"

He flipped open the top of the doughnut box and grabbed one of the raised doughnuts before spinning the open side of the box towards Jamie and nodding to him to take one as well. Jamie looked at Abigail, not sure if he was the intended recipient of the treats. She could hardly say 'no'. She gave him an almost imperceptible nod and he reached for a cake doughnut.

"I have big plans for this place. Do you realize we have entered the money making time of the year? December is the month that can make or break a small business. And I intend to put The Thinking Bean on the map this year. No more screwing around!" He lifted his doughnut into the air like he was talking to an audience, then bit into it with relish.

Zeke had a history of rash and unusual activity. There was no doubt he was smart, Abigail thought he was smarter than both her and their Mom, and probably even smarter than their Dad, which was saying something. He'd been accepted to every college and university he'd applied to, and received scholarship offers from all of them. When he chose Dartmouth, she alone had wondered how he would do so far from home. When he dropped out in his second year, everyone else had wondered why. It was never a huge mystery to Abigail.

Her brother liked learning, loved books, lived for discussion and debate, but was the biggest softie. She'd always known his heart was with his family and the people he loved. He wasn't really cut out for the pressure of high academia. In that way he was very much like their father, who had carved out a nice life as a high school counselor even though his intellect could have taken him much farther in the field of psychology. Their Dad was happier in a close community helping people. She wasn't surprised Zeke had chosen, similarly, to stay in their home town.

"What are you planning?" She asked. Jamie gave a little laugh that sounded more like a snort and Abigail shot him a look.

"Mistletoe Madness," Zeke announced into the air above their heads, holding his hand up, palm out, and sweeping it slowly from left to right as if he saw the words written on a giant sign high on the opposite wall. He paused for effect, then looked at them both with a gleam in his eye.

Jamie groaned. Abigail waited for some further explanation from Zeke. He took an aggressive bite of his doughnut, making his hair flop crazily into his eyes. He flipped his head back dramatically to put it back in place and chewed at her with a confident grin on his face. She shifted her gaze to Jamie who gave her a weak, apologetic smile.

Turning her attention back to her big brother, she asked, "What, exactly, is Mistletoe Madness?"

Chapter Four

"Mistletoe Madness is a genius marketing plan I have devised that will entice customers into this place, bring the community together, create the biggest and best holiday celebrations this town has ever experienced, and make me a ton of cash!" Zeke stood as he spoke, stretching his long arms wider and wider, and raising his voice with each word. When he didn't receive a response, he looked down at Abigail and Jamie, waving his hands up and down like he was trying to get them to applaud.

Abigail and Jamie looked at each other. Jamie gave her a half-shrug as if to say, "See what I have to live with?"

"Music!" Zeke's eyes flew open and he dashed to the counter, putting one hand on the shining surface and throwing his feet and legs over, landing on the other side with a flourish. He ducked down so only the top of his head was visible and must have pushed an unseen button, because acoustic guitar music suddenly filled the room.

A car pulled up in front.

"Customers!" Zeke announced happily. "Talk amongst

yourselves. I've got this," he told them and began pulling cups down from the shelves in preparation.

Abigail and Jamie looked at each other again. She was confused, but she sincerely doubted she would get any clarification from Jamie. She took a sip of her cappuccino and watched as a middle aged couple she vaguely recognized entered the coffee shop.

"Randy, Jill!" Zeke greeted them warmly. The couple smiled at him and went to the counter to place their order.

As Zeke chatted with the couple and the soothing acoustic guitar filled in the quiet, Abigail stared at her drink. Jamie shifted uncomfortably in his chair. She hoped he would just quietly eat doughnuts until Zeke was back. The thought of walking in on him mostly naked was more embarrassing when her brother wasn't there as a distraction. Jamie cleared his throat and she knew he wasn't going to remain silent. He had always done the opposite of what she wanted him to do.

"You glad to be home for Christmas?" Jamie asked.

Great. Now she had to talk to him.

"Yes, of course," she answered. She barely looked at him as she responded, then went back to staring at her cup. A new humiliation came to her mind. Jamie must know that she'd been fired. Zeke knew, he'd even said so when he greeted her upstairs. She scowled. Discretion was impossible in this little town.

"So, um, sorry about earlier. I didn't know—" he started to say.

"Let's not talk about it, okay?" She interrupted crossly.

"Sure, right," he bobbed his head up and down.

Zeke was still chatting up his customers at the counter. Abigail wondered if Jamie would leave soon, maybe go to work? But then she remembered Zeke said he'd been laid off. She glanced at him sideways. He was tapping the handle of his coffee cup, looking awkward. Abigail felt a little bad for snapping at him. It wasn't his fault she'd barged into Zeke's apartment unannounced.

"So..." she started.

He perked up and looked at her, leaning forward.

"You're living with Zeke?" She asked.

"Yeah, yeah," he head bob nodded again.

"How's that going?"

"Oh, you know..." He glanced at Zeke who was talking animatedly behind the counter, keeping Randy and Jill laughing. "It's always exciting." He switched his gaze to her and grinned.

She chuckled a little. Zeke was nothing if he wasn't exciting.

"You're not working?" She ventured the question.

"Well, I've been staying pretty busy helping him with some projects around here. Shelves and lighting, that kind of thing. And I've been doing a few handyman jobs around town," he explained.

"That's nice."

There was a short pause, then he continued, "I got laid off last year. Zeke really helped me out letting me stay with him."

She could sense a humbleness in his tone. He'd stopped tapping his cup. His hand, now still, lay quietly on the table.

"I just got laid off...or let go, I guess," she said, a little surprised at her own confession. A surge of emotion moved through her and she was mortified to realize that her eyes were wet with tears.

Jamie watched her, concern on his face, "That sucks, Abby." He had such an empathetic look on his face, she couldn't bring herself to reprimand him for calling her 'Abby'.

"Well, what can you do?" She brushed the tears away with the back of her fingers.

"Yep, you just gotta keep going," he said. They sat

awkwardly for a moment, then Jamie moved the doughnut box towards her, offering her another one.

"No, thanks."

"You want another drink?" He made like he was going to stand up and make her another cappuccino.

"No, thank you," she gave him a small smile so he would know she was okay.

He smiled back. His big, crooked, dopey Jamie smile, but Abigail found it almost comforting this time. Familiar.

"Are you helping with Mistletoe Madness?" She asked, hoping to change the subject.

Jamie leaned back in his chair, his shoulder's slumping in defeat, "Yes."

"He's Santa," Zeke informed her as he joined them back at the table. Randy and Jill waved to all of them as they left with their coffees.

"Santa?" Her mouth pulled into a smirk. She looked at Jamie for verification. He wouldn't look up, just sighed and nodded in agreement.

"I can't be Santa, because I'll be too busy," Zeke explained. "I need someone who can focus on the role while I take care of everything else."

"I see," she said. Although she didn't, not really.

"I'm going to be a Snowman," Zeke declared.

"I don't understand what's happening," Abigail cracked up a little as she spoke.

"I told you, Mistletoe Madness! We're going to host weeks of events and parties and special decorations leading up to the big day," Zeke explained. "I've got a band lined up and all kinds of stuff. Oh!" He grabbed her arm, "You can paint the windows."

"What?"

"You know, with that white snow looking paint. Make something really festive, something totally unique." He was so excited, it was difficult not to fall into his enthusiasm a little bit.

Abigail turned her attention to the floor to ceiling windows in the front of the store. It would be fun to create something beautiful on them. She'd never really thought about painting on glass.

"I guess..." she answered.

"See? You getting fired is a blessing in disguise. You can work for me!"

Abigail squirmed a little bit at the 'fired' comment. Although, if painting was involved in this little adventure maybe it wouldn't be so bad. She could earn some money while she was searching for the next big move in her career. She took in a deep breath, the smell of coffee mixed with books was a good smell. Since he'd turned the heat on, it was starting to warm up a bit. Her eyes wandered across the funky little space Zeke had created. An elaborate version of Jingle Bells played on acoustic guitar filled the room.

"What do you say?" Zeke waited, his eyes hopeful.

"Sure," she answered. "Why not?"

"Great!" Zeke moved his big hand to her shoulder and pushed her back and forth, making her sway in her chair. "Mom's working on the costumes."

"Is she?"

"Santa," Zeke pointed at Jamie, who resigned himself to the role with a brief nod. "Snowman," he pointed at his own chest. "Elf," he turned his long finger towards Abigail.

"Elf? What?"

"It's too late, you already took the job!" Zeke stood up and started stacking their used cups in one hand to carry to the sink.

"You didn't say anything about wearing an Elf costume," she argued.

"You have to wear a costume," Zeke told her.

"Why?"

"Tell her," Zeke said to Jamie as he stepped away from the table.

Jamie let his head flop back and sighed in the way of the long-suffering soul who carries a heavy burden.

"Tell her," Zeke commanded as he walked away.

Jamie let his head loll to the side to look at Abigail. When he spoke, he kept his face slack, like a zombie. Speaking in monotone, he told her, "Because it's Mistletoe Madness."

❄

"COME ON, SWEETIE," her Mom waved to her from the other side of a wall of elderly women, motioning her to hurry up.

They were in Needle Point, the Pitkin Point craft store that was stuffed full of bolts of material suitable for Elf costumes as well as Christmas craft supplies. Today was a 50% off sale. They had come to pick up some sewing supplies to finish the Santa, Snowman and Elf costumes that Abigail's Mom was making. Abigail had agreed to help her mother, but she had not expected the madness that a 50% off sale could inject into a geriatric craft crazy crowd.

Luckily, her Mom was brutal in these situations. She hurried and leaned and pressed her way past even the most aggressive little old ladies in order to get the material she wanted. Abigail was too afraid of stepping on someone's toes or, heaven forbid, knocking a fragile grandmother over and having her break a hip. So she hung back, letting her Mom get what she needed while she waited. Apparently her Mom was now done and wanted Abigail to get to the other side of the crowd where the cash registers were busily ringing up half-off purchases.

Abigail made a face at her mother. She was not good at

crowds. She certainly wasn't good at pressing her way through crowds.

"Go around," her Mom instructed as she made wide circular motions over her head like she was twirling a lasso. "I'll get in line for the cashier," she said before turning her back on Abigail's situation and joining the long line of crafters waiting on the cashiers.

Abigail looked for a way around. Up until now, she'd stayed relatively out of the way by backing up against the wall of 75% off Thanksgiving supplies, which were not in high demand, plus the wall was mostly empty of any products. She stood on her toes and spied a path along the Thanksgiving wall, through the wedding section, which she assumed would be in low use at this time of year, then to the front door.

Within a few minutes she was waiting for her Mom outside in the parking lot. It was freezing cold, but she preferred that to being in the crowded store.

The door of the pizza place next door opened. She knew this because someone had attached sleigh bells to the door so they jingled every time it opened and shut. It had opened and shut a half dozen times since she'd escaped the craft store. Often enough that she'd stopped paying attention.

"Hey, Abby," a familiar voice called.

She turned to see Jamie walking towards her with a sullen teenage boy trailing behind him. Jamie wore a brown Carhart jacket and a black hat pulled down over his ears. She was struck again by how much more manly he looked these days. He had never been small, he was at least a few inches taller than her, not quite as tall as Zeke, but he'd never looked quite this strong. It wasn't just his size, though. Something else was different about Jamie Turner. He looked...competent.

"Hi." She smiled thinly at him.

"Are you all right?" Jamie looked around, presumably for a car with a flat tire or dead battery. Why else would someone stand around in a parking lot in sub-freezing temperatures as night was falling?

"I'm fine. I'm waiting for my Mom, she's in there," Abigail jerked her head towards the craft store.

"Oh," Jamie noticed the stream of little old ladies leaving the store with multiple bags. "Wow, they're really busy," he said.

The boy, maybe 13 or 14-years old, was shuffling behind Jamie, his head bent over the glowing screen of a cell phone. Jamie stepped aside and put his hand behind the boy, presenting him to Abigail.

"This is my son, Dillon," Jamie said with more than a little pride in his voice.

Son? Abigail searched her mind for any information about Jamie having a son. She supposed she had heard something about it at some point. He had married Raegan Faller after high school. Zeke had been his best man. She remembered Zeke telling her about it when she was away at college. And she remembered they had divorced some time ago. Yes, she had heard about him having a son. But that was a baby boy. This was an almost adult human standing in front of her.

"Dillon." Jamie waited for the boy to respond. He didn't. He just kept thumb typing into his phone. Jamie looked at her, "Sorry." Then he took his palm and lightly bopped the boy on the back of his head. Dillon looked at him angrily. "Dillon, this is Abby, Zeke's sister," Jamie said. Then he glanced furtively at Abigail before continuing, "And my friend."

The introduction took Abigail a little by surprise. So much so, she decided not to correct Jamie about her name. Not in front of this surly young man who obviously didn't care who she was. Not when he'd just called her his friend.

"Nice to meet you, Dillon," Abigail said.

"Nice to meet you," Dillon mumbled, giving her the

briefest look before staring at the ground in front of him. He remained off of his phone, but didn't attempt any further engagement.

"He looks so much like you," she said without thinking. Jamie smiled and ducked his head, taking it as a compliment, which it was.

It was also true. Seeing Dillon standing in front of her kicking at the asphalt brought back memories of Jamie when they were kids. Besides his hair being a little lighter in color than Jamie's had been, Dillon was the spitting image of his Dad. The skinny, gawky, uncomfortable Jamie she had grown up with. Dillon's attitude seemed to be about the same, too.

"Here I am," announced her Mom in a sing-song voice.

They turned to see her mother approaching them, laden down with several bags stuffed with everything she would need to finish their costumes. Abigail's Mom was almost as tall as her daughter. Slender, with dark, straight hair she kept cut in layers, and swooped up in the latest fashionable look. She had a thin nose, high cheekbones, full lips and wide set, narrow eyes. Abigail had received almost all of her mother's features, but she'd always felt like they settled better on her Mom's face than on her own. Her mother's face was open and confident where Abigail's always looked pinched and morose.

"Hello, Jamie," she said warmly.

"Hello, Mrs. Ackerman," Jamie said. He reached out for her bags, "Let me help you with those."

"Thank you," she said, letting Jamie take them. Then, seeing Dillon, her eyes lit up, "Dillon! My goodness you've grown! You're turning into quite the handsome young man."

What might have been a smile flickered across Dillon's grim expression. He nodded and said something unintelligible.

"You two need to come over for dinner soon," her mother said as she popped the trunk for Jamie to deposit the bags.

"Thank you, that would be very nice," Jamie answered, glancing at Abigail as he said it, as if the invitation had been her idea.

Driving home in the car, Abigail watched out the window as they passed yards full of Christmas decorations, her Mom chattering on and on.

"He's had such a rough time, that Jamie. Such a nice boy. And his son! Could you believe how big he was? He's going to be taller than his Dad soon I bet," she paused to take a breath.

Abigail continued staring out the window. She, too, was having a hard time thinking about Jamie having a child so near to being grown up. It was strange, seeing him act like a Dad. Like her own Dad acted.

Her Mom glanced at her sideways, "He's handsome, too. Wouldn't you say?"

"Dillon?" Abigail asked, confused.

"No, Jamie," her Mom responded, giving Abigail a meaningful look.

"No, I don't know, I guess," Abigail turned to her Mom. What was she trying to say?

"Well, I think he's handsome. And he's the nicest boy."

Abigail scoffed, "He's not a boy and he's not as nice as you think he is."

"What do you mean?"

"He's, you know..." Abigail searched for the words and couldn't find them.

"He's always polite and such a hard worker," her Mom offered evidence for her opinion.

Abigail scoffed again, "He's not always polite, Mom."

"Oh? When has he not been polite?"

"When we were kids! He and Zeke were always playing jokes on me, being mean."

"Oh, well, honey, that's just kid stuff." She carefully

steered the car around the last corner before their house. "Besides, it was mostly Zeke playing jokes. Jamie was always falling all over himself trying to get your attention." She made a 'tsk-tsk' sound. "He was such an awkward boy, and so in love with you."

Abigail heard the words, but couldn't exactly process the information. She stared at her mother, her mouth agape. What a ridiculous thing to say.

A burst of laughter came out of her so hard it turned into a snort. "Jamie Turner is not, and has never been, in love with me, Mom."

Sarah Ackerman gave her only daughter an amused nod and a knowing smile. "Whatever you say, sweetie, whatever you say."

Chapter Five

Abigail balanced on a plank of wood placed across two eight foot ladders, a cup of white paint in one hand and a paintbrush in the other. The ends of the plank were stuck through both ladders right above the fifth rung, adding over five feet to her height and allowing her to reach the upper most regions of the coffee shop windows.

She wore a large, white apron over her Elf costume, which consisted of red tights and a bright green belted tunic with a red and white long sleeve shirt underneath. She also had bright green and white striped Elf shoes and a green Elf hat with a fat, red tassel, but she'd left those on one of the tables to avoid getting paint on them. She felt ridiculous enough wearing this costume. Besides, her hair was having an unfortunately frizzy day and she worried that the Elf hat just exacerbated that look.

The sounds of Zeke and Jamie having a loud discussion behind the coffee counter filtered through the Christmas jazz music Zeke had chosen for this morning's ambience. Abigail glanced back at them and found a silver lining in this whole

Mistletoe Madness experience. She may look ridiculous in her costume, but they looked even more ridiculous in theirs.

Jamie wore the classic Santa Claus suit, complete with pillows stuffed under his jacket and cinched with a wide, black belt, to make him look plump and jolly. His red Santa hat had a white Santa wig sewn to the bottom so when he took the hat off, the Santa hair left with it. He also had a huge, white curly beard that fixed over his ears, which he wasn't wearing at the moment. It was tucked into his black belt for safe keeping and easy access.

Zeke's costume, however, took the cake. Abigail had to give her Mom kudos for the ingenious way she'd built his Snowman suit. With wire forms, she'd made what was once just a long, white triangle of material with giant black pom-poms affixed to the front for buttons into a Snowman looking body that puffed out from Zeke in all directions. He had a white hood that he pulled up over his head and a black top hat that fit over the hood. He wore black tights on his legs and a long sleeve black shirt, giving the Snowman stick like arms and legs. He also had a bright red and green striped scarf wrapped around his neck.

He was identifiable as a Snowman. However, his extremely long limbs seemed even longer sticking out of his puffed up body. And his beard added too much hair to the look. Plus, with the added girth to his normally lean frame he had already had a few accidents. His Snowman butt had pushed a bag of sugar off of the counter, spilling it all over the floor. And already one cup had been lost to the same fate, making an even bigger mess.

"I can't eat with the beard," Jamie was arguing.

"Santa doesn't eat," Zeke told him.

Jamie scoffed at the stupidity of that statement, "Well, this Santa eats. I'll put it on as soon as I'm done with this." Jamie held up a half a bagel smeared with cream cheese,

"Anyway, how do you think Santa got his jolly look?" He pushed his rounded belly towards Zeke who gave him a scowl.

Zeke was tense. They were one day into decorations for Mistletoe Madness and he was a man under pressure. He'd put so much thought and energy into this idea, he was going a little crazy, like Zeke had a tendency to do.

The day before they had all been fitted for their costumes. Then they strung little white lights in every nook and cranny of the bookstore. There were houseplants with long, delicate vines that hung all throughout the narrow reading areas. They twisted white lights carefully through the vines, giving the cramped areas a festive, almost fairy like appearance.

"When did you get all these?" Abigail had asked, letting her eyes drift across all of the plants. Zeke didn't' have a green thumb to her knowledge.

"They're Jamie's," Zeke, whose hands were busy holding on to an extra long vine while Abigail fixed lights on it, used his forehead to point at Jamie.

"Yours?" She asked Jamie.

"Yeah, I have a little plant addiction," he answered. "I had to bring them with me when I moved in. We thought they looked good here."

Abigail nodded in agreement, "Nice."

Jamie took the compliment with an embarrassed head bob. For a moment she thought about what her Mom had said in the car and wondered if it could be remotely true. Was this goofy awkward head bob thing Jamie always did a residual effect of some long ago crush he had on her when they were kids? She thought about all of the stupid pranks he and Zeke had played on her, the way he'd always laughed when she got mad and yelled at them, and the way he'd barged into her 18th birthday party and mocked her for not having a date to her senior prom. No, she decided, her Mom was mistaken.

Abigail had drawn up a design for the window painting which included snowflakes and elaborate curlicues across the top, turning into elves and presents and sparkly books down the edges. Then a sweeping snow scape across the bottom that included all kinds of adorable woodland creatures wearing hats and scarves, and reading books. She left the large center section empty of design, because Zeke wanted to build a Christmas tree by stacking old books into a cone shape and then decorate it with lights. He'd insisted that he wanted the book tree visible through the glass.

He'd also insisted she wear her Elf costume while painting.

"It will look like we're actually in Santa's workshop!" He had told her, delighted with the idea.

So now she was a real, living, breathing Elf on a Shelf in the window of The Thinking Bean, painting snowflakes and listening to her brother and Jamie bicker. She couldn't help but smile at the oddness of it all.

"Abigail," Zeke called to her.

"What?"

Zeke pushed his Snowman body past Jamie's Santa body and squeezed out from behind the counter. He headed towards the front window. Jamie followed him, grinning at his view of the Snowman outfit from behind, and chewing his bagel.

"I scheduled a meeting in the morning at the library," Zeke informed them.

"What meeting?" She asked.

"To organize Mistletoe Madness," he answered, exasperated with her ignorance. He let his stick arms droop to his sides like someone fighting a losing battle.

Abigail looked at him, "Why the library? Why don't we just have the meeting here?"

Zeke chuckled as if she was a foolish child. Abigail caught

a flash of humor cross Jamie's face as he watched the back of Zeke's head. She crinkled her brow at him, what was the joke?

"We need to meet somewhere else, so we can focus," Zeke explained.

"Tell her the real reason," Jamie nudged the middle of Zeke's back.

Zeke shook him off, "That is the reason."

"That's not the reason," Jamie responded, taking another bite of his bagel and moving to one of her ladders, leaning lightly against it as he chewed. He was facing Zeke now, and he looked up at her, his eyes twinkling with merriment at making Zeke uncomfortable.

Abigail turned around, placed her paint can and brush on the wood plank, and sat down so she was facing them. Her red Elf legs were hanging off the edge of the plank. She swung them like a little kid.

"What's the real reason?" She asked.

Zeke tried to stare them down, which was impossible when he looked like an angry, bearded marshmallow.

Jamie swallowed and said again, "Go on, tell her."

"There's nothing to tell," Zeke argued, but his voice had lost its commanding tone.

"Tell me what?" Abigail wanted to know.

"Want me to tell her?" Jamie teased.

Zeke threw his long stick arms into the air in defeat, "Fine, tell her."

Jamie turned his attention to Abigail. When she looked down into his face his eyes were dancing, ready to share a joke, and she felt a small tingle of excitement.

"One word," he said, "Fern."

Apparently the new librarian at their small county branch was named Fern. And apparently Fern was younger than the previous librarian, much younger, with short, stylish blonde hair, a pretty face, and a perky, fun attitude. And apparently she was wicked smart and well read, and Zeke had something of a wild crush on her, and was always coming up with reasons to go to the library these days. All of this was according to Jamie, but none of it was denied by her brother, who paced uncomfortably around the room in his Snowman costume while Jamie told Abigail all about it.

"So I like her? What's wrong with that?" Zeke defended himself as he rearranged the bagged coffee bean display with agitation, his top hat slightly askew.

Abigail, amused at the idea of her wildly confident and outgoing brother having a sweet, old fashioned crush on a librarian, shrugged and smiled, "Nothing's wrong with that." She looked down at Jamie for confirmation who was chuckling as he took a sip of his coffee.

"No, nothing wrong with that at all," he agreed. Then he winked at her, and Abigail felt another little thrill.

She stopped thinking about Zeke for a moment and considered her reaction to Jamie. He looked more than a little ridiculous in his Santa outfit, especially without the beard. But as she watched him pop the last bite of bagel into his mouth and chew while eyeing Zeke with a highly amused expression, she realized that she felt attracted to him. Physically.

How was that possible?

Her mother's comment had gotten under her skin and now she was having a major overreaction to Jamie Turner. That's how. Sheesh.

"Customers!" Zeke called out, happy for the distraction.

Jamie turned to see who was coming as he reached to his belt for his Santa beard. Suddenly, his amused expression fell and he looked tense, guarded. He didn't take the beard out of his belt, but he did glance quickly up at Abigail as if he was expecting something to happen. What, she didn't know.

The door opened, jingling the sleigh bells they had affixed

to it yesterday while decorating. Abigail turned just in time to recognize Dillon stepping in the door.

"Dillon," Jamie moved towards his son, who was gawking at his father. The boy looked like he was halfway between cracking up laughing and wishing he could leave.

Behind Dillon, a tall woman with curly, blonde hair cut just above her shoulders, and a slightly shorter man, who was nonetheless wide shouldered and fit, followed close behind. They almost ran into Dillon because he had stopped short upon seeing Jamie's Santa outfit and not left them enough room to enter.

"No dilly dallying...Dillon," the man said, laughing at his alliteration. At the sound of his voice, Abigail immediately knew who he was, though she hadn't recognized him by look alone. Blake Thompson.

"Mom," Dillon stepped away from the woman when she gently placed her hands on his shoulders. An attempt to move him out of her and Blake's way.

Mom. Abigail's mind clicked everything into place. This was Raegan. Tall, gorgeous Raegan who used to be a brunette, and was now a blonde. Who used to be married to Jamie, and now was not. Mother to Dillon and...married to Blake Thompson? Abigail suddenly recollected that she had heard that bit of gossip during some distant conversation in the past. Blake Thompson. She thought again what she had thought then, who in their right mind would marry Blake Thompson?

"Dad, what are you doing?" Dillon was still staring at Jamie with that special blend of humiliation and contempt that teenagers have down to an art form.

"I'm Santa," Jamie said, lifting his arms out to his sides as if showing off more of the costume would help his son understand, or forgive, him. It didn't do either.

"Dillon, come here and get your drink," Zeke called to the

boy over the sounds of the espresso machine. Dillon made for the counter, bypassing Jamie.

"Really, Jamie? Santa Claus?" Raegan said, the snide tone impossible to ignore.

Abigail felt the hackles on her neck rise. She'd never liked Raegan, and she really didn't like the way she was looking down her nose at Jamie in his costume and, by association, Zeke.

"Abby?" Blake had spotted her on her perch and moved towards the makeshift scaffolding, smiling his car salesman smile.

She was surprised to be seen, but then realized that was silly. Did she think she was invisible just because her feet weren't touching the floor?

Raegan turned her attention to Abigail and let her gaze slide up and down her huge apron with the Elf tunic underneath. Abigail wished she was having a better hair day. She wished she was wearing something a little more intelligent. She wished she was doing something more...big city. One side of Raegan's upper lip twitched into something that was not quite a smile, "Abby, wow, I didn't know you were back in town."

That was a lie, Abigail was almost positive.

"Abigail, I go by Abigail," Abigail corrected them.

Raegan and Blake exchanged a look.

"Of course, Abigail" Blake said, smiling at her with gleaming teeth.

Raegan's eyes wandered down Abigail's costume to her shoeless, red tight covered, feet. She opened her mouth to say something.

"I'll drop him off tonight, then?" Jamie interrupted. He had returned to the ladder just next to Abigail, closer in fact. The presence of him in his bright red jacket was oddly comforting. Abigail trained her eyes on him and didn't look back at the other two. Maybe she could avoid a conversation by denying them any eye contact.

It worked.

Jamie conversed with Raegan about when Dillon needed to be taken home and what their schedule was for sharing custody over the next week. It seemed congenial, but Abigail sensed it wasn't. Not completely.

Blake had lost interest. Because she wasn't allowing him to catch her eye, he meandered over to the counter and ordered two lattes. When she was sure everyone was engaged and not paying any attention to her at all, Abigail allowed herself one furtive look. Blake stood next to Dillon with his arm around the boy's shoulders. She noticed that Dillon was equally averse to Blake being chummy with him as he had been with Jamie. She was happy that Jamie wasn't the sole recipient of Dillon's ill mood. Blake had taken off his winter hat and Abigail noticed that he was completely bald. Another win for Jamie.

She looked away, down past her feet dangling off of the wooden plank and to the floor. What did it matter to her if Jamie was getting along with his son, or competing in any way with Blake Thompson? She had no interest in his personal life. Not really.

Abigail peered at Raegan, careful to keep her head down and look as if she was still staring at the floor. Jamie's ex-wife was still beautiful. Raegan had a strong, firm body. She'd played volleyball and basketball in high school and was always very good. Her medium length blonde hair was curled loosely and complimented her heavy jaw. She was dressed like someone with money. She'd always dressed that way, probably because she came from a family with lots of money. She was, however, not a kind person in Abigail's opinion. There were countless incidents she could remember of Raegan, and Blake for that matter, being awful to her or someone else in school.

Bullies. And now they were married and probably bullied the world together.

Abigail's gaze slipped back to Jamie standing near her feet. He looked tall and strong from this perspective. She could see the muscle in his jaw flexing as he listened to Raegan complain about something and deduced he was gritting his teeth. His hair was messy from when he'd taken off his Santa hat, but it was thick and wavy. Again, she felt a small victory for him in that fact.

She curled her toes a little inside the red tights, they were getting cold. The voices of everyone else blended into the background as Abigail withdrew into her thoughts. They weren't thoughts, really, more like emotional memories of her childhood.

She remembered how excited she would get when Zeke and Jamie invited her to go with them somewhere, anywhere. How her friends, few that they were, would swoon over her brother and his friend when they were at her house. How, when things were good, the boys had made her laugh harder and longer than anyone else ever could.

She glanced up and took in the scene of Jamie having a tense conversation with his ex-wife while dressed like Santa. And Zeke, his Snowman outfit causing him fits while making coffee and serving from behind the counter, politely and confidently holding his own against one of their town's notoriously obnoxious men. And her, she looked down at her red and white striped arms and thought about how silly this all must look to someone like Raegan. And she didn't care.

A sense of pride and camaraderie swelled in her chest and Abigail decided that she was glad to be working here, helping her brother, on the same team with Jamie, and doing her part in the gloriously over the top festivity of Mistletoe Madness.

Chapter Six

The next morning, while their mother watched the shop, Zeke, Jamie and Abigail convened at the library meeting room to focus on the details of Mistletoe Madness. Zeke did not dress like a Snowman. In fact, he dressed pretty snazzy for someone who was merely going to the library. He smelled extra good, too.

When Abigail saw Fern she understood why.

Fern was petite, but had an air of smart and sassy. She dressed pretty hip for Pitkin Point wearing loud, floral tights and a black skirt with layer upon layer of shirts, sweaters and scarves, all in varying shades of teal. She had a short, funky blonde hairdo, which Abigail suspected might be dyed pink or blue if the locals were less conservative. She was naturally pretty and didn't wear much makeup, if any, underneath her dark purple rimmed glasses. Her blue eyes sparkled when she saw Zeke, so much so that Abigail shared a look with Jamie, who gave her an I Told You So eyebrow raise.

"Did you close down the shop?" She asked, her voice pleasant and perky.

"My Mom's watching it for us," Zeke answered. Abigail

detected a slight crack in his baritone and had to contain her smile. Her brother had it bad.

"This is my sister, Abigail," Zeke said.

Fern's face broke into a perfectly lovely smile, "Well, hello, Abigail. I've heard a lot about you."

"Have you? Anything good?" Abigail took Fern's offered hand warmly. She liked her.

"You've been recruited for Mistletoe Madness?" Fern asked.

"No getting around it, I'm afraid," Abigail answered. She wondered just how much time Zeke spent with Fern. She seemed to know a lot about his life for a mere crush. "Have you been? Recruited, I mean."

Fern motioned to them to follow her. "Of course," she laughed and the sound of it mixed with the jingling of a bunch of keys that hung from a lanyard around her neck, making her movement seem like it was accompanied by bells.

"Fern's going to help with Christmas poetry reading night," Zeke said excitedly.

Abigail heard a sigh escape from Jamie.

"Not into poetry?" She asked him.

"Some of it. But I have a feeling poetry night might be a long night for ol' Santa," he answered.

Fern showed them to the meeting room and left them to their planning. Zeke had come equipped with an oversized calendar and colored markers. Until the moment she saw him plotting out a Christmas cupcake decorating party with an orange marker, Abigail hadn't completely understood how seriously he was taking this whole Mistletoe Madness thing.

Not only was the cupcake party planned for tomorrow, with flyers having gone out to the local schools and churches as well as the YMCA, but he had ideas for a bookstore scavenger hunt date night, a children's book reading of selections like How the Grinch Stole Christmas and Bear Stays Up for

MISTLETOE MADNESS

Christmas for which he'd hired a few actors from the local theatre company, poetry night, of course, and he was trying to find a horse and wagon for some old fashioned hay rides around town. All of this was going to culminate with the Christmas Eve dance that Pitkin Point always held outside at the gazebo in the park, rain or snow—or freezing ice storms. Abigail was impressed.

"Fern suggested a Dicken's night, where we read parts of A Christmas Carol and maybe get some of the church choir to come as carolers," Zeke told them, his excitement building.

"When did Fern tell you this idea?" Abigail was curious.

"Oh, when we were out the other night," Zeke answered.

Abigail raised her eyebrows, "Are you and Fern a thing, Zekey?"

Zeke's face turned red under his beard and he completely ignored her, which told her everything she needed to know.

"He's afraid to jinx it," Jamie informed her.

"Don't talk about it," Zeke said, still staring at his colorfully marked up calendar.

"This is so cute," Abigail said. "Does Mom know?"

"No!" Zeke looked at her now, "Don't tell Mom, not yet. I'll tell her when it's time."

"Okay, okay." Abigail grinned, pleased to see him this way. It would be nice for Zeke to find someone, and judging from her first impression, Fern seemed like a good fit.

"I really think that we can pull people in and get them to finally branch off from the town square for once," Zeke said, changing the subject.

The citizens of Pitkin Point were notorious for staying within what was referred to as The Town Square, a two block area that included Main Street, and basically ignored businesses outside of that area. All of the town's best restaurants and retail shops were inside The Town Square. Main Street was lined with old fashioned lamp posts that were hung with lights and Christmas wreaths, giving it an extra special appeal during the holidays. Even though The Thinking Bean was only a few blocks outside of The Town Square radius, it may as well have been on the other side of the world.

"I think you have a shot," Jamie said.

"A shot at Mistletoe Madness working or a shot with Fern?" Abigail asked. Zeke glared at her.

Jamie grinned, "Both."

"Enough! Let's get organized. We can't leave Mom manning the shop forever," Zeke said. To keep him from having a melt down, Abigail and Jamie turned their attention towards event planning instead of matchmaking.

❄

The Christmas Cupcake Decorating Extravaganza was a big hit. Kids, young and old, came to decorate twelve dozen cupcakes that Take the Cake provided at cost. Zeke and Jake put up a long lunch table that they borrowed from the school down the center of the coffee shop section to hold the cupcakes and all of the frosting supplies. Judy had delivered the plain cupcakes and stayed to give advice on how to decorate them with panache.

The coffee shop was packed with children and their parents, and the book sections were abuzz as they browsed and picked out Christmas gifts. Their Mom manned the cash register, while their Dad helped customers find books. Jamie's Santa chair was set up in the front corner of the coffee shop. Abigail stuck to her Elf job and assisted him by keeping the line of children waiting to see Santa as orderly as possible, and by wiping their hands and faces with wet wipes to avoid getting frosting in his Santa beard. He was wonderful with the kids, patient and kind, Ho-Ho-Ho-ing like a pro.

MISTLETOE MADNESS

Zeke was in his element. As a host he was marvelous, welcoming everyone, directing them towards what they were looking for, encouraging them to decorate a cupcake, happily making espresso drinks for the grown-ups. As a Snowman, he was a little less impressive.

He still hadn't mastered total control over his puffy rear end and Abigail witnessed several incidents where it came into contact with the head of a small child or the cupcake they were holding. Once he turned to greet someone at the door and bumped two cupcakes off of the center table onto the floor. As a result, Zeke's Snowman behind was blotted here and there with brightly colored frosting. She hoped their Mom had some killer ideas on how to clean his costume.

Dillon was there to help as well. Raegan had dropped him off after school and he'd ended up helping Abigail's Dad in the book section. There was an old fashioned wooden rolling ladder that could be used to reach the top most shelves, and Dillon had taken charge of it. He was the official climber, fetching books for people and monitoring the little kids who were drawn to the ladder like it was a toy. When he wasn't getting books, he gave the kids careful, slow rides on the ladder back and forth between the cupcake table and the book sections.

Old fashioned Christmas carols by Dean Martin, Bing Crosby and a few by Elvis set the mood. As Abigail watched the semi-chaotic festivities, the children laughing, the parents happily buying books as gifts, the smell of sweets and rich coffee and mocha drinks filling the air, she thought it really did seem like...well, like Christmas.

"Your Dad is really good with Dillon," Jamie said to her. There was a lull in their Santa line and Jamie was sitting back, observing, like her.

Abigail glanced to where her Dad was talking to Dillon by the ladder and, surprisingly, Dillon was laughing and talking back to him. His face had lost its teenage angsty look and he seemed bright and happy. She looked back to Jamie who was watching the scene with a smile in his eyes, which was all she could see because of his beard.

"Dillon does look like he's in a better mood, today," she said.

"Oh, he's usually in a good mood...with everyone but me and his Mom," Jamie said with a small sigh.

"I guess that's a teenager thing, isn't it?"

"Yeah, I suppose it is. Probably a divorced parents thing, too."

There was a pause as they both watched Dillon. When he was light hearted and chatty, he was quite a good looking young man. He really did remind her of Jamie when he was young. A question popped into her head, but she wasn't sure Jamie would want to answer it.

"It's none of my business," she began, "and you don't have to answer, but do you and Raegan get along? Or was it a nasty divorce?"

Jamie looked at her then thought for a moment before he answered, "It wasn't pretty, that's for sure. It was such a long time ago, though. Dillon was only two. So it's better now. I've just never lived up to what she wanted me to be, and she's not shy about letting me know how she feels about it."

"What did she want you to be?"

"Rich," he laughed a little, as did Abigail. Then he got more serious, "I worked construction out of high school, which is good money...when there's work. And we were so young, we probably should have never gotten married to begin with, we were very different."

Abigail nodded, but remained quiet. Her eyes drifted between watching Dillon and watching Jamie as he talked.

"I got hurt at work right after Dillon was born. Things just went downhill after that." He lifted one shoulder in a half-hearted shrug. "Things weren't too bad, though. I couldn't go back to construction, not like I did before I was hurt. So I worked at the hardware store and concentrated on being a good Dad."

She smiled at that. Putting aside the fact that he liked to tease when he was a teenager, it seemed like he'd mellowed out quite a bit now that he was grown. It wasn't difficult for her to think of him as a good Dad.

"I'm sure you're a good Dad. What are you going to do now that the hardware store is closed?"

He dropped his gaze. "I don't know, exactly, besides doing odd jobs. Fixed up the gazebo for the town council." He watched her and there was weighted meaning in his eyes. "Do you remember when we used to go to the gazebo?"

Memories of them at the gazebo in the early morning, before the park was officially open, and watching the sunrise came to her. Then more memories of being there late at night. She recalled that the goal was to be at the gazebo when nobody else was there, when they weren't supposed to be there either. She didn't remember Zeke, just her and Jamie. For some reason the thought of it made her feel shy.

"I remember going there a few times," she answered, looking down at the floor.

Jamie watched her, his eyes focused and still holding an emotion that she couldn't quite read. The space between them filled with something almost electric. After a few moments he glanced away and released her from his gaze. When he looked back he was normal old Jamie again.

"What about you?" He asked.

"Me?"

He leaned forward in his chair, pulling his Santa beard down so it hooked underneath his chin. "Yeah, do you think you're gonna stay here? Do you like being a graphic designer?"

It was Abigail's turn to do a half-hearted shrug. "I don't

know what I'm going to do. I'm not sure I want to stay in graphic design. It's interesting, but dealing with clients is awful."

Jamie nodded in understanding.

"I do know one thing, though," Abigail continued. "I'm not staying here."

Jamie's eyebrows lifted under his Santa hat. "No?"

She shook her head to bring the point home. "No, I'm not into the whole small town thing."

"Oh." He looked around at the mellowing cupcake party. His head bobbed up and down slightly as he considered her comment. When his eyes moved to the windows that she'd painted, he paused. He tilted his head at the window and asked, "What about painting? You've always been an incredible painter."

Abigail followed his gaze to the window decorations and scoffed a little. "That? That's just messing around. It's not real painting."

Judy, whose cupcake table had finally emptied, approached them with a great sigh of relief.

"That was crazy fun wasn't it?" She asked.

"Yes, it was," Jamie answered.

"Zeke said you did this," Judy was talking to Abigail, but pointing at the window decorations.

"Yes," Abigail nodded.

"Do you think you could do it for the bakery?" Judy asked.

Abigail didn't know what to say. Jamie's eyebrows lifted again as he looked first at Judy then at Abigail.

"I'd pay you," Judy added.

Jamie smiled and nudged Abigail, giving her his I Told You So face. Abigail still didn't know what to say.

"It's just so beautiful, and I was thinking maybe you could make something sort of similar, but with little elves baking?

That would be cute for a bakery, don't you think?" Judy continued.

"That would be real nice," Jamie said, smiling at them both.

Abigail was flattered, and flustered, but Judy waited patiently for an answer. Finally, Abigail gave her a small nod.

"Sure, I could do that," she said.

"See?" Jamie said happily after Judy left, "I'm not the only one who thinks you're talented!"

Chapter Seven

After the wild success of the sugar-filled, child-focused, Christmas Cupcake Decorating Extravaganza, Zeke was unstoppable. His plans for the Holiday Poetry Reading expanded to include hiring a local teenage girl who was one of the best cellists in the state as extra entertainment. In addition to selling coffee and snacks, he decided to offer free wine to the adults, figuring this would loosen them up to read poetry as well as make purchases.

"As long as you don't let them leave with it," Charlie, one of the two deputies Pitkin Point paid to patrol their quiet town, instructed him.

Charlie was just a few years older than Zeke and Jamie. They'd all gone to school together. Abigail had gone to school with Diego, the other deputy. He'd been a few years behind her.

The two deputies perfectly complimented each other. Where Charlie was broad and fair, Diego was lean and dark. Where Charlie was a stickler for the rules, Diego was more likely to let you off with a warning.

"Of course," Zeke readily agreed to Charlie's conditions.

Since The Thinking Bean didn't have a liquor license, technically they couldn't serve wine. But Charlie was willing to let it slide since it was a special occasion and Christmas, but he explained to Zeke that anyone receiving wine would have to be over 21-years old, and they couldn't leave the premises with the alcohol.

"I'm serious about this, Zeke," Charlie's ruddy cheeks darkened as he warned her brother. He wasn't a fan of Zeke's over the top personality, though they had always been decent to one another. Charlie was thick and heavy with a wide face made even wider by his blonde buzz cut. He was old fashioned in his thinking, but a solid cop. He just wasn't necessarily in for all of the shenanigans that Zeke had always been prone to creating.

"I know you're serious, Charlie," Zeke gave the deputy an agreeable yet sternly competent face.

"We'll keep an eye on it," Jamie added, putting his hand on Charlie's shoulder. Charlie looked at Jamie's hand then at Jamie, but didn't crack a smile.

"See that you do," he said. Taking his coffee to go, Charlie left the scene, shaking his head in vague disapproval as he did.

With that begrudging go ahead, Holiday Poetry Reading Night at The Thinking Bean was on.

Since this was more of an adult, evening type affair, Zeke agreed to ditch their costumes for the night.

"As long as you dress up," he instructed as Jamie and Abigail high-fived each other. Abigail was happy to gussy up a bit after wearing her Elf costume for days.

She spent the afternoon at Take the Cake, visiting with Judy and painting their window with some Christmas fun. After they came up with the initial design, the painting only took her a few hours. Judy gave her a crisp $100 bill and a lemon meringue pie. Not bad for an afternoon's work.

Abigail ate a pleasant early dinner with her parents with the pie for dessert. Then she headed down to Zeke's old room to change. She took a quick shower, avoiding getting her hair wet so she wouldn't have to blow it dry. Blow drying really brought out the frizz in her hair. Letting it get steamed up in the shower, however, gave it extra curly bounce.

She dressed in jeans, black suede boots, and a black, form fitting, off-the-shoulder sweater. She found a silver and rhinestone snowflake necklace that her Mom had given her years ago that she'd hardly worn. Along with the matching snowflake earrings, the necklace added just the right amount of Christmas to her casual, beatnik look.

The Thinking Bean was abuzz with activity when she arrived. She counted at least a dozen people in addition to her parents. Zeke was there, and Fern, who looked lovely in black tailored slacks and a tight fitting jacket with a V-neck that was trimmed in faux black fur. Jamie was nowhere to be seen.

"Lookin' good, sis," Zeke beamed at her from behind the counter.

"You're just used to seeing me in an Elf costume," she quipped. "Where's Jamie?"

"He went to pick up Dillon," Zeke answered. He lifted up two bottles of wine for her to choose, "Red or white?"

"I'll have white," Fern said, stepping up to the counter next to Abigail.

"I love your sweater," Abigail told her. Fern's smile lit up her brilliant blue eyes as she thanked her.

"One white," Zeke handed Fern a glass of wine with what Abigail noticed was a flirty and extended look. "What'll you have, Abbah Dabbah?"

"Red, please," she answered.

"Make that two," Jamie's voice came out of nowhere from just behind her shoulder.

Abigail turned around to tell him he'd scared her, but as soon as she laid eyes on him, she struggled to remember what she was about to say.

Maybe it was because of the little white lights that decorated the coffee shop. Maybe it was because he was standing so close to her, close enough she could smell his cologne, and it smelled good. Or maybe it was because she'd been looking at him in his overstuffed Santa outfit for the past few days, but Abigail was shocked into silence when she saw him.

He had that just shaved look that made her want to reach out and touch his cheek. He wore a burgundy corduroy long sleeve shirt with the top few buttons undone, and a pair of jeans with boots. His hair had a messy, just got out of bed for a photo shoot kind of vibe, and there was a glimmer in his blue eyes. Eyes that seemed particularly blue tonight.

"Hi," she said, because she realized her mouth was hanging open.

He smiled and she noticed something that she'd never really noticed before, Jamie Turner had dimples. He ducked his head before looking up at her, a little bashful, "You look beautiful, Abby."

The tiniest thrill tumbled through her stomach at the sound of him saying her nickname. That, combined with the look in his eyes and the fact that he smelled so good, made her decide not to correct him. Just inches away from each other, a memory of him in his towel flashed through her mind and she blushed.

"Two reds," Zeke said.

Jamie moved to take both drinks. As he did, there was a silent exchange between the two men that Abigail couldn't put her finger on. Of course, her hormones were reeling from Jamie's body skimming past hers to grab the wine, the closeness of him overtook all of her senses. She started to say something to Zeke, wanting him to explain, break up these feelings, offer her some protection. But Zeke kept his eyes trained on Jamie and vice versa until Zeke gave his friend an almost imperceptible nod. It was that man nod that men do to one another when they are acknowledging something from the secret man club. It was a move she'd seen men do countless times but never really understood the social cues surrounding it. Understanding or not, Abigail knew something was different now that it was done, and that it had to with her. As if Zeke was giving permission to Jamie to...what, exactly?

The moment was gone in an instant and her brother turned to help another customer, leaving her with Jamie. And even though the small room was full, when he shifted his attention back to her she felt as if they were completely alone.

"Your wine," he said, offering her one of the glasses. When she lifted her hand to take it, her arm brushed against his. He didn't move, just watched her, his eyes smiling. Abigail wrapped her hand around the wine glass and, without meaning to, covered his fingers with hers as she did. He didn't pull his hand away, probably waiting until she had a good grip on the wine glass. Probably.

"Thanks," she managed to say. Her mouth felt dry and it made her voice sound hoarse.

He lifted his glass to hers and clinked it, leaning towards her so she could hear him over the cello music and chatting customers. He was so close she could have easily turned her face and kissed his cheek.

"Cheers," he said. His voice was low and deep, rippling across her shoulders and neck.

Abigail couldn't speak, she just lifted her glass and took a sip. Jamie did the same, keeping his eyes locked on hers. Try as she might she couldn't look away from him. He was literally attracting her, holding her attention. And for reasons she could not understand, she liked it.

"This is pretty," he dropped his eyes to her throat where the snowflake necklace sparkled. He lifted his hand and put his finger under the pendant, balancing it on his fingertip to see it better. His touch was light, but enough for her to feel the warmth of his skin on hers. So gentle. Abigail felt her breath quicken and the heat rising in her neck and cheeks.

"Ladies and gentleman, can I have your attention please," Fern's lilting voice rose above the murmur of conversations, breaking whatever moment was happening between her and Jamie. Abigail turned to face the front corner of the room, which had been Santa's area and was now the poetry reading corner. Even with her back to him, Abigail could still feel Jamie's presence. He wasn't touching her, but for some insane reason she kept thinking about him touching her. She took a sip of her wine and absently fingered her snowflake pendant, the warmth of his touch on her throat still distracting.

Thankfully, Fern was in full control of Holiday Poetry Reading Night. As a librarian, lover of poetry and literature, and one of the most open minded and lyrical people in their midst, she was a perfect choice to MC the event. With nearly 30 people now sitting in the cafe area or wandering through the book sections, there was an air of nervousness when she invited anyone in the room to kick off the event by volunteering to go first.

There was no way Abigail was going to get up in front of an audience of any size and recite poetry. It just wasn't in her. Apparently nobody in the room was feeling any braver, because Fern's invitation was met with an uncomfortable silence.

"I'll go," Zeke spoke up from behind the counter. He glanced at Abigail and gestured towards the cash register, a silent request for her to run the counter for him. She changed places with him and he made his way to the corner. Though he must have been at least a full foot taller than Fern, somehow they looked really good next to each other. Like a team.

Zeke pulled a sheet of paper out of his pocket. He'd come prepared.

"Since this evening is a holiday themed event, I've chosen to read Good King Wenceslas by John Mason Neale. I'm not going to sing, so you can all relax," he said. A few chuckles broke the silence.

Reading the lyrics turned out to be quite beautiful, especially with Zeke's deep voice and spirited interpretation. The crowd broke into applause when he was done and he swept his long arm behind him as he bowed low.

"Now," he stood up, beaming at his audience. "Who's next?"

A number of people got up to read Christmas or holiday poems. Abigail kept busy behind the counter, refilling wine glasses or selling goodies, even making drinks, though she tried to do that in between readings since the noise was distracting. She was able to enjoy her mother's recitation of Christmas Eve: My Mother Dressing, and Miss Pearl, a retired school teacher who was probably the oldest person in town, reading The Oxen by Thomas Hardy.

During one break, Dillon approached the counter with a five dollar bill in his hand. His shyness was palpable and she wondered if he would bolt out the front door if she said the wrong thing.

"What would you like?" She asked with a smile.

"Um, a chocolate chip cookie...please," he managed, holding the money out to her.

"Oh, don't worry about it," Abigail waved the bill away. "It's only fair that Santa's son gets a free snack every now and then."

Dillon kind of laughed and she figured a half laugh was better than nothing. Abigail reached into the back of the glass counter and grabbed the biggest chocolate chip cookie they had with a thin tissue. Bent over, she thought she heard Jamie's voice from the far corner of the room. She stood up and caught Dillon looking at her with surprise, then they both turned to see Jamie taking his place at the poetry reading corner.

"I don't have a Christmas poem," he began, Zeke and a few of the others booed, only teasing. "But," Jamie held his palm up towards the hecklers, "I do know one poem by heart. So I figure that's the one I should do."

"You know a poem by heart?" Zeke called out to him, still joshing.

"I do." Jamie scanned the room. He looked nervous until his eyes fell on Dillon and he relaxed a little bit, smiling. "I memorized this poem in high school." His gaze moved past Dillon to Abigail, where it held for a few beats, long enough for Abigail to feel that tingling excitement she'd had earlier return. "It's called 'She Walks in Beauty'," his face broke into a huge, goofy Jamie smile, then he looked back to the crowd, "and it's by Lord Byron."

For the next few minutes nobody asked for a refill or a snack, which was good, because Abigail was captivated by Jamie's recitation. The whole room was, in fact. Not having to read while he spoke, Jamie made eye contact with the audience. A hush fell over the room as he recited the beautiful words, a starry eyed tenderness on his face.

On the last line, he caught her eye again and she was held hostage to his look, unable to think or move or even breathe for a few moments. His voice ended and a lovely silence filled the space, as if everyone was afraid to move or speak. Then several people turned to see what Jamie was gazing at with such adoration. Their attention broke whatever was connecting Abigail to him and she quickly averted her eyes, staring at the floor at her feet, blushing furiously.

Dillon turned back, really looking at her for the first time, his face full of curiosity. Before anyone could say anything, Abigail shoved the chocolate chip cookie at him, blurting out a hushed, "Here you go. Excuse me." Then she fled to the book section and out the back door into the alley.

The night air was cold, below freezing, and her breath plumed in front of her face as she paced up and down the alley. She was too angry and embarrassed to be cold. The back door clicked open and Jamie leaned into the alley, lit by a triangle of light.

"You okay?" He asked.

Abigail stopped pacing and turned on him. "What was that about?"

Jamie glanced back inside the bookstore then stepped all the way into the alley and let the door shut behind him. They were now bathed only in the blue light of the moon and the washed out glow of a distant streetlamp.

"What was what about?" He asked.

"That!" Abigail waved her hand wildly at the door. "What were you doing in there?"

Again, Jamie looked to the bookstore, then back to her. He shoved his hands into his pockets, bewildered at her anger yet sensing he was supposed to feel guilty. "A poetry reading?"

Abigail scoffed, "What's with all the...googley eyes and 'You look beautiful, Abby' baloney?"

Jamie was stunned at her jabs. In truth, she was too. She wasn't sure why his poem had brought on such wrath, but she didn't want to figure it out. She wanted him to take it all back and stop acting like such a buffoon.

"I didn't mean to make you mad," he began.

"Well, you did," she snapped at him, crossing her arms tightly across her chest.

"I–it's just–" he fumbled for words, which annoyed her even more.

"You what?" She asked impatiently.

"That poem always reminded me of you," he confessed. He looked down at his feet, shuffling them like he used to when they were young, like his son did now. "I wasn't trying to make a big deal about it. I thought I was being nice," he said.

"Like when you made a joke about asking me to prom? That same kind of nice?" Abigail spat the words at him before she even knew they were coming out of her mouth.

He stopped shuffling and looked at her with surprise. She couldn't blame him. She was surprised herself.

"What?" He looked puzzled.

"When you barged in and made fun of me for not having a date for prom at my birthday party," she said, the memory of it flooding back. Her 18th birthday party. The pink and purple balloons festooning the table her parents had reserved for her and her few friends at the fanciest Italian restaurant in town. How grown up she'd felt. How special. Then Jamie bursting into the room wearing a ridiculous black wig and fake mustache, singing Happy Birthday to her like an opera star, asking if she had a date to prom in a stupid Italian accent. The whole restaurant had watched him, laughing at him, at her, at them. She'd been mortified.

For a few moments he didn't say anything, just looked into her eyes, his breath like chugs of steam that floated past his face and up into the moonlit night.

"It wasn't a joke," he said.

It was Abigail's turn to be stunned. Finally, she managed, "What?"

"It wasn't a joke," he said once more.

"It wasn't a joke?" She asked. Her mouth was getting dry again.

"No," Jamie let his eyes follow the curves of her face, lost in some memory. "I wasn't making fun of you. I wanted to take you to your prom." He ducked his head for a long time. Then came back to the present and lifted his eyes to her. "Apparently I wasn't very good at asking." He broke his gaze away from her face and looked around the alley, letting out a frustrated sigh. "Apparently I'm not good at any of this."

"Any of what?" Her heart was pounding, anger and confusion mixing together inside of her chest.

He shook his head, "It doesn't matter." He shoved his hands deeper into his pockets and raised his shoulders up towards his ears. "It's freezing out here. You should get inside."

A shiver went through Abigail's stomach, but she didn't know for sure that it was caused by the cold.

Chapter Eight

They were called Fivedust and their equipment barely fit into the front half of the cafe section of The Thinking Bean. A local indie rock band, the only decent local indie rock band according to Zeke, Fivedust had agreed to do a gig two Saturdays before Christmas and include as many Christmas songs as possible on their song list. They also offered to lead the audience in Christmas carols as a finale to their performance. Zeke was in seventh heaven.

After the resounding success of the Cupcake Extravaganza and Poetry Reading, word had spread through Pitkin Point and beyond about the fun and festive events at The Thinking Bean. If the line forming at the counter and winding its way all the way out the front door this Saturday night was any indication, it seemed Mistletoe Madness was working its magic.

"Where are we going to fit everyone?" Zeke wondered, his eyes alight with excitement.

"Dillon and I can get those extra chairs out of the basement," Jamie said.

"If we took out some of the tables we could fit more chairs in here," Abigail suggested.

Zeke snapped and pointed first at Jamie, "Do it!" Then he did the same to Abigail, "Great idea!" Though her brother had once again relaxed the staff costume requirement for this evening's event, Zeke had taken a liking to his Snowman top hat and wore it now with his street clothes. Abigail thought he looked like a mix of Abraham Lincoln and a character straight out of a Charles Dickens story, but he still managed to come across as kind of cool and fairly intelligent. She had to hand it to him, despite his sometimes zany ideas, her big brother was kind of an impressive guy.

The big table and chair move began. Zeke took care of the line of customers while Jamie and Dillon retrieved chairs from the basement and took the tables that Abigail moved out of the cafe area.

Unfortunately, the close quarters and number of customers in the room made it impossible for her to ignore Jamie, which she'd been successfully doing since their conversation in the alley. Not ignore exactly. More like keep things professional or pretend that nothing intimate or embarrassing or hurtful had taken place between them.

"Sorry," Jamie said. Their shoulders had bumped accidentally when he was carrying a stack of chairs past her just as she straightened up from pushing a table towards the back.

"It's okay," she said politely. Her voice sounded calm, but she wanted to scream at him to not apologize, to stop being so kind, to man up and be offended or irritated or aloof. That would have been preferable. It would have been a normal reaction after how she'd treated him in the alley. But not Jamie. He lived his life, apparently, to be a thorn in her side.

At first he'd been a reminder of the embarrassment she'd felt when they were young. Now the sight of him made her rethink everything she'd ever believed about him, every assumption she'd ever made about his behavior. And it made her wonder if her reactions over the years had been justified or cruel. When she looked at him Abigail felt like she'd just kicked a puppy. And that was not a good feeling.

"Dad," Dillon stuck his head into the cafe from the book section of the store. "There's just a few more down there, I'll get them." He disappeared, leaving Jamie standing next to the stack of chairs he'd just put down. Uncomfortably close.

"Need some help?" Abigail asked.

"No, I got it," he answered as he grabbed a chair from the top and set it on the floor. "Thanks," he added. Unrelentingly polite. Infuriating.

Fivedust started their gig at 6:00 pm, which was early for a band, but not so early for people who frequented coffee shops. The music was good and really loud in the small space. People were crammed wall to wall, sitting and standing, sipping their hand made refreshments. Zeke had not been able to convince Deputy Charlie that free wine at this event was acceptable. A poetry reading was one thing, but a "rock concert" with alcohol that might find its way into the gentle, quiet streets of their small town was too much of a risk.

It turned out that this was a good call on Charlie's part, given how the evening turned out.

As Fivedust performed to The Thinking Bean's packed audience, the temperature in the shop became unbearably warm. Zeke asked Jamie to prop open the front door and the back door that led to the alley in order to let in some of the arctic air from the mid-December night. This action had two unforeseen results.

First, people who were a little late to the concert weren't dissuaded from entering the shop because they could easily hear the loud music outside on the red brick sidewalk. They ducked in and got a hot drink, then enjoyed the music happily from outside. Second, the customers who got tired of sitting in the too warm building wandered out the front door to mingle with others on the sidewalk, or out the back door to take cigarette breaks in the alley. All the while Fivedust's music carried from the coffee shop out into the quiet night.

Fern had joined Zeke behind the counter and there wasn't a lot of room for anyone else to assist. Besides, Zeke seemed happier when Fern was around and Abigail didn't want to invade on their space.

The growing crowd on the front sidewalk drifted across the street to the park. The Southeast corner of Pitkin Point's beloved City Park was nicely situated near The Thinking Bean. It looked charming, too, with a number of park benches, old fashioned street lamps festooned with giant Christmas wreaths, and the quaint gazebo that had been dressed up for the season with pine boughs, huge red velvet bows and white lights of its own.

Given there wasn't a lot she could do to help at the moment and she didn't want to take up room inside where a paying customer could sit, plus the fact that she felt the need to avoid Jamie if possible, Abigail decided to go to the park. She discreetly retrieved her black wool coat from the coat rack near the door, pulled it on outside and wandered over to the gazebo.

It was beautiful. She hadn't spent much time at the park since coming home. She'd been too busy with Mistletoe Madness. But it had been one of her favorite places when she was a kid. One of their favorite places, her and Zeke...and Jamie.

The music floated through the clear night air and added to the mood. Fivedust was currently playing a beautiful version of Have Yourself a Merry Little Christmas that they'd dressed up with their own style. She took in a breath of the fresh, cold air and let out a sigh as she walked. It was the first time she'd had a few minutes with nothing else to do in a while. This was exactly what she needed, some time by herself enjoying the night and forgetting her problems.

The last snow had come just after Thanksgiving and remnants of it were still scattered in the shadiest parts of the park. There had been talk of a big snowstorm possibly heading their way soon and Abigail hoped it would. If she was going to be in Pitkin Point for Christmas, at least it could be a white Christmas.

She smiled at a few people who had made themselves comfortable on one of the benches while they listened to Fivedust. It was remarkable how clearly their music traveled on this clear night.

Abigail noticed that nobody was in the gazebo, so she decided she'd pop inside and get the full effect of the Christmas decorations from its higher vantage point. As she gripped the handrail and trotted up the stairs, she was startled to find Jamie sitting on the bench seat opposite her. She hadn't seen him from the path as she approached.

"Oh!" She put her hand on her heart.

Jamie stood up, holding his palm out to her like she was an animal he didn't want to frighten, "Sorry."

She took a few deep breaths. "It's okay."

"I thought I'd take a break. It's hot in there."

She nodded. "Me too. It is, isn't it?" She laughed, out of nerves more than humor.

Jamie nodded. He glanced around at the empty benches along every wall of the gazebo. He took a step forwards, then backwards, then did a half turn and stopped again, never once looking her in the eye.

"Well, I'll leave you to it," he said and sort of lunged towards the top of the stairs where she was standing, trying to make a quick exit.

"You don't have to leave," Abigail blurted out.

He stopped a few feet in front of her and lifted his gaze.

When she looked into his eyes it felt as if someone was squeezing her heart. There was sadness in his eyes and longing, and worst of all a loneliness that she recognized. She'd seen the same look in her own reflection. Abigail reached out and touched his chest, as if her hand alone could keep him from pushing past and leaving.

"Please don't go because of me," she said, so quietly she wasn't sure she'd even spoken the words out loud. Except she was sure, because she saw him relax. Felt him relax.

He had a question, she could read this much on his face, but he didn't ask it. A group of concert goers walked by, talking and laughing. Jamie glanced at them, let his eyes follow them as they passed, then looked back at her.

"Okay, I'll stay," he said.

She pulled her hand back and pushed both of her hands into her coat pockets.

"Do you want to sit down?" Jamie gestured towards the bench seating. She shook her head 'no'. He nodded, his head bobbing up and down like it did when he was nervous. A smile pulled at the corners of her mouth.

"It's beautiful isn't it?" She said, moving to the edge of the gazebo and looking out over the park. The moon was high in the sky, and the tiny white lights hung all around them on the gazebo, as well as on each wreathed street lamp. They looked like sparkling gems placed by magical Christmas elves.

"Yes, it is," he answered, stepping next to her, but leaving a more than comfortable distance between them. Those few extra inches squeezed her heart again. What she'd said to him, what she'd thought about him all these years, had put an invisible wedge between them. And that made her sad. For the briefest of moments Abigail thought she might tear up, but she blinked hard and managed to keep her cool.

"Do you remember the Christmas Dance when Zeke and I were seniors?" Jamie asked. He was looking into the middle distance, focusing on a memory, his hands in the pockets of his dark brown jacket.

Her mind clicked back through several memories of the Christmas Dance here in the park. It was a wonderful yearly celebration with a bonfire, fresh kettle corn made in a giant cast iron kettle, hot chocolate and hot apple cider, music, everyone dressed up and wrapped in their warmest and finest. It had only been snowed out twice as she was growing up. The people of Pitkin Point welcomed snow at the Christmas Dance and only shut it down when it veered towards blizzard conditions. She tried to remember Zeke and Jamie's last year in high school.

"I think so," she said, recalling some specifics. "It was kind of warm that year, wasn't it?" She remembered that detail because she could picture the dress she had worn. A midnight blue dress with long sleeves and crystals sewn into the bodice. She remembered she'd found blue sparkly tights that matched and had been thrilled she didn't have to cover up the dress with her coat during the whole dance.

Jamie nodded, glancing at her, "You had on a blue dress."

She looked at him in shock, "You remember my dress?"

He nodded again and chuckled, "I had it bad for you, Abby."

"You did?" Again, shock.

"I bought boxes of mistletoe and hung it all over inside this gazebo." Jamie pointed up and down the eight beams that stretched out from the center of the gazebo to the edges. "I was trying to make sure to get you under the mistletoe." He shook his head and chuckled again at his youthful determination. He looked at her sideways, his eyes crinkling at the corners with humor. "Not that I would have known how to go about kissing you under the mistletoe if it had worked."

Abigail's mouth hung open with surprise at this story. A story she'd never heard, "Jamie, I had no idea!"

"I know," he answered.

She took a few moments to think about what he'd said. Then her brow wrinkled with confusion. "Why didn't it work?"

"Well, a lot of guys noticed you that year, I guess. You spent the whole night on the dance floor. You never came up here."

She did remember dancing a lot that year. She'd always attributed it to the fact that it was so warm and everyone was dancing.

"I didn't come up here once?"

"Not once. I waited."

She pondered his answer, then asked, "Why didn't you ask me to dance?"

Jamie sucked air through his teeth, "Dancing? That wasn't a thing when I was that age." She laughed at his reaction and he smiled at her again. "I guess I lost my nerve."

"Oh." Abigail travelled back to that night and thought about Jamie waiting for her in the gazebo, too afraid to ask her to dance. It was so sweet and sad. She tried to read his expression as his eyes drifted across the moonlit park and the happy couples enjoying their impromptu outdoor concert.

"That was the night I decided to ask you to prom. Of course, I chickened out that year. But I finally got up the guts the next year for your senior prom..." he chuckled again, but there wasn't much humor in it this time. "And we both know how that turned out." He shook his head and looked away from her.

"Jamie, I–" she began.

"No, I'm not telling you all this so you can feel sorry for me," he interrupted, turning back to her and raising his palm up as if warding off her pity. "I just want you to know that there was zero chance I was trying to make fun of you or embarrass you in any way when I did that. I just wanted us to be square on that point."

She didn't say what she'd been about to say, which was that she was sorry she'd fled in embarrassment from him at that Italian restaurant, left him without an answer. She'd only done it because she really didn't know he was asking her to prom. She would have said 'yes' and they would have gone and had a great time. If she'd only known.

Abigail stood mute, looking into his eyes, and realized that he wanted to end it this way, on sure footing. There was no reason to dive into all of their teenage angst and misunderstandings. It's not like they were a couple or going to be one.

"Okay, we're square," she said.

He waited for something more. When it didn't come, he nodded curtly, finalizing the deal. "Okay, good."

A few moments went by, the space between them filled with unspoken words. Her heart squeezed again, but Abigail didn't pay it any attention. This wasn't high school and there was no row of mistletoe hanging over their heads. This was reality.

"Friends?" She asked, or rather, demanded.

He didn't look away from her, just stared right into her eyes. The muscle on his jaw flexed as if he was biting his tongue, then he started to answer, but his voice caught. He cleared his throat, "Okay, friends."

And that was that.

Chapter Nine

"What do you mean I have to be his date?" Abigail asked. Zeke, wearing his tophat, towered over her in their parent's living room.

"He also has to be your date. It's mutual," Zeke explained, sort of.

"I don't see why I need a date or why he needs a date at all," Abigail argued.

"It's the Mistletoe Madness Bookstore Scavenger Hunt Date Night," Zeke said, raising his arms so they were even with his shoulders, like he was a ringmaster in a circus.

"Why don't you want to go with Jamie?" Her mother asked. She was sitting on the couch, knitting a sweater from a large ball of bumpy, olive green yarn.

Abigail didn't want to get into a discussion about Jamie with her mother. She glared at Zeke, who was blissfully ignorant of how touchy this situation was for his two top, only, staff members.

"It's not that I don't want to go with him, I just don't understand why Zeke thinks we should go together," she tried to explain.

"You're the only two people who know how the scavenger hunt is supposed to work, besides Fern and I. You need to be each other's dates so you can lead by example," Zeke told her.

"Do you have someone else to go with?" Her mother asked.

"No, Mom, I don't," Abigail felt her resistance crumbling. She sighed, then asked, "Did you already tell Jamie?"

"Yeah, he's down with it. No problem," Zeke answered.

"I like Jamie," her Mom interjected.

Abigail had a headache.

"His son's a good kid, too," their Dad got in on the conversation, speaking out from his chair where he'd been reading a book. Being the high school counselor gave him final word on the goodness or badness of any given teenager in town.

"You know, sweetie, it wouldn't kill you to go out with him on a real date," her mother said.

"Mom!" Abigail felt like she was 13-years old.

"Not Dillon, of course, but Jamie," her mother said.

"I knew you didn't mean Dillon," Abigail said. "Can we talk about something else, please?"

"All right, you don't have to get upset," her mother turned to Zeke, who had sat down in one of the wing chairs with his long legs stuck out in front of him, crossed at the ankles. "So you and Fern are getting pretty serious, aren't you?"

❄

THE SCAVENGER HUNT Date Night was the most complicated of the Mistletoe Madness events. It had taken all four of them, Abigail, Zeke, Jamie and Fern, several hours each afternoon for three days to come up with the scavenger hunt list, create the printouts and rules, and decide on the prizes.

Basically, a couple would arrive at the bookstore and mark the time they started the scavenger hunt on their printout. They would be allowed 90 minutes to find as many things as possible on the list. Then they would turn in their printout with the time they finished written on it. At 8:00 pm the printout would be reviewed for accuracy and the winners chosen.

First prize was a dinner for two at Ming's Golden Palace, the best Chinese restaurant within 50 miles. Second place was dinner for two at the pizza place. Third place was two tickets to the movie theater. Five runner ups got a $10.00 gift card to The Thinking Bean, and everyone else who entered got a $5.00 off $10.00 purchase at The Thinking Bean. The questions ran the gamut from 'Find a book about what you wanted to be when you grew up' to 'Find a book with the word Rock in the title' to 'Find a book about a robot', and so on.

Any other time, Abigail would be happy to take part in this kind of scavenger hunt. It was intellectual and lighthearted all at the same time, and something she would normally enjoy. But now that she and Jamie had been paired together as the example date for other patrons to emulate, she felt nothing but nervous.

To make matters worse, stupid Zeke refused to lift the costume requirement for this event. He was in his full Snowman gear and she and Jamie were stuck as Santa and his Elf. At least, she thought, that might make it seem less like a real date and more like work. Fern had agreed to be Zeke's date and, in the name of getting into the spirit of things, was dressed as a Penguin.

"What about this one?" Jamie held up a sci-fi book with a robot on the cover.

"What's it about?" Abigail asked, moving closer to him so she could see the description on the back of the book.

They had begun the scavenger hunt, choosing to go first and get it over with while Zeke and Fern ran the counter. Then they would switch places.

"It's not about a robot," Jamie said, sliding the book back into place. "Which begs the question, why is there a robot on the cover?" Sarcasm was thick tonight.

One thing none of them had thought about was that The Thinking Bean was a rare and used bookstore, so the titles were often obscure and little known. Even when you could think of a book that fit the scavenger hunt question, it was not always a book that was in the store. So far, Abigail and Jamie had been hunting for 30 minutes and had only filled in two of their questions.

Jamie made a frustrated growling sound, "This is hard." He skimmed over the printout in his hand and pointed to one of the questions, incredulous, "Find an author who has the same name as your middle name? Find a book with 394 pages?!? Who came up with these questions?"

"We did," Abigail said, laughing a little at his outburst, which was made all the more amusing because he was dressed like Santa.

"Right." He slumped comically against the wall. "I would rather face a line of little kids who want to give me their Christmas lists," he whispered just loud enough for her to hear.

She laughed again, "I thought this sounded fun, but it is a bit tedious, isn't it?"

He nodded at her, his Santa beard askew. Without thinking, she reached out and tugged on one side so it was even. A look flickered across his eyes, but it was so fast Abigail couldn't be sure she'd actually seen it. She dropped her hand and he cleared his throat.

"Quite a few people came," he said, looking away from her and towards the other couples in the book section.

John and Judy were there. Nannette and Pete, who owned the pizza place, were also there. Deputy Diego had brought his wife, Marissa. He was in street clothes. In fact, all of the couples were in street clothes. Except her and Jamie.

When their 90 minutes were up, they had only managed to answer five of the 30 questions on their printout, and they were exhausted. As they took over the counter from Zeke and Fern, Jamie gave Zeke a hard time.

"If anyone can answer all of those questions in 90 minutes we should give them more than a Chinese dinner."

"Let's see how many we can do," Zeke said to Fern.

"Right on," she answered, giggling.

They turned and strolled arm and arm towards the books. One tall, spindly limbed Snowman and a short, beautiful Penguin. They offset each other and created a perfect match. Abigail was happy for her brother, she truly liked Fern. But watching them saunter off so content, so in tune with each other, just made her feel depressed.

"You good?" Jamie asked from his position at the espresso machine.

"I'm fine," Abigail said, turning towards the next customer.

Maria Cortez, Abigail's high school Spanish teacher, was waiting with her elderly mother at the cash register to place their order.

"Oh, Abigail, you look adorable in that costume. I heard you had moved back to town," Maria, or Mrs. Cortez as Abigail had always called her, exclaimed warmly.

"Hi, thank you. I'm just back for the holidays. Not staying forever," Abigail said. She felt the need to clarify her plans to anyone and everyone. Especially herself.

"Oh, that's a shame. It would be nice to have you around again," Maria smiled so kindly when she spoke. She had always been kind.

"It's good to be home for Christmas," Abigail admitted.

"Can my mother and I play this game?" Maria asked, noticing the scavenger hunt printouts on the counter.

"Of course," Abigail responded.

She and Jamie continued to work close together behind the counter, often bumping lightly into each other, especially with his extra large Santa body in the way. They were good at reading what the other person needed and getting orders out fast, even though they did it with very little conversation. Inside, Abigail felt tight, like her neck and shoulders were binding up and her stomach was pulling together in knots.

With all of the customers, the little shop got very warm again. She was hot in her long, striped sleeves and tights. She glanced at Jamie, who still sported his Santa hat and beard. He must be boiling. He didn't complain, however. He kept working.

When the scavenger hunt was over and the printouts were being reviewed, Jamie excused himself.

"I've got to get out of this suit," he told Zeke. "I'm cooking in here."

Zeke nodded, "Sure, man, go ahead."

And he was gone.

Abigail spent some time helping look over the printouts, but after a while Zeke and Fern seemed to have a system going and she felt like a third wheel. She looked at the clock and realized Jamie had been upstairs for almost 45 minutes. She had assumed he would return, and as each minute passed and he didn't appear, Abigail was more and more distracted. Was he okay? Had he gone into Santa costume induced heat stroke?

As soon as the winners were decided, she told Zeke she was going to take a break and he nodded his approval. A minute later Abigail was climbing the narrow, antique stairway up towards the apartment. She hadn't been up there since the first day she'd surprised Jamie getting out of the shower. This time it was dark. Very dark. There was no light on in the stairway or on the landing and she didn't know where the switch was to turn it on.

As she moved up the stairs her stomach fluttered with...something. Nerves? Excitement? Was she actually worried she might find him having a seizure on the floor?

At the landing she felt her way to the door and hesitated. Maybe he didn't want company. Maybe he specifically didn't want her company. She almost turned around, insecure about how he would respond to seeing her at his door. Then she stopped. They were friends, right? That's what they'd agreed. A friend could check up on a friend, couldn't they?

She took a deep breath to stay the terrible shiver of nerves in her stomach and knocked on the door. Not too soft, not too hard. The knock of a friend.

The deep tones of his voice muffled through the door, "Hang on." She heard movement, then the door handle turning, the door pulling open, dim light from inside the apartment spilled into the hallway onto her Elf costume. "It's not locked–"

He stopped. He was expecting Zeke, of course. Not her.

"Hey," Abigail gave him an awkward little wave.

"Abby," he said, as if he needed to say her name to make her real. She felt relief at the sound of her nickname. It meant he didn't hate her.

He was out of his Santa costume, his hair going in all directions as if he'd pulled the wig/hat off quickly and left it at that. He wore a green T-shirt and casual black workout pants. He looked tousled and casual and extremely sexy.

"I...um, I wanted to–" she fumbled for words, unable to explain her presence there in his personal space.

"Do you need me?" He asked. She knew he meant downstairs in the shop, not literally. But she felt her heart thumping in response.

"No, no, it's not that. I was just checking on you."

There was a long pause as he studied her face. Her vision adjusted to the low light and she could see the outline of his jaw, his biceps and shoulders, his hand holding the top of the door. Suddenly, unbidden images of Jamie wearing only a towel flitted through her mind and her heart thumped hard again.

He pulled the door open and stepped to the side. "Want to come in?"

Yes. She did.

He closed the door behind her and motioned to the couch, "Have a seat."

Abigail sat down on one side of the worn, comfortable couch. There was a lamp on in the corner of the room. It gave off a low, warm glow. Jamie went to a second lamp and reached for the switch, intending to turn it on.

"Don't," Abigail said. He stopped. "You don't need to. It's nice in here. Relaxing."

He sat down on the other side of the couch and turned towards her. Abigail let her head move back and rest against the cushion. Enveloped in the quiet of the room with Jamie's presence so close by, she wanted to sink into the cushions and stay there.

"Rough day, wasn't it?" He asked.

"Mm-hmm," she murmured.

"I don't know why tonight was so hard," he wondered out loud.

Abigail thought she knew, but she didn't want to say. Her eyelids felt heavy and she fought the urge to close them. She turned her head on the cushion so she could look at Jamie, so solid and calm.

"I'm sleepy," she admitted, letting her eyes close before opening them slowly again.

"Then sleep," he said. Abigail felt a warmth move through her body and she relaxed. Remarkably, without thinking any more about it, she drifted off to sleep.

When she woke, minutes or hours later, she couldn't be sure, she was in the exact same position. Jamie had moved. He was facing forward, his feet on the coffee table, the back of his head resting on the couch as he looked thoughtfully at the ceiling. He must have heard her stirring, because he turned his head and grinned at her.

"I'm sorry," she said, the fog of sleep lifting slowly from her brain.

"It's okay, you must have been tired."

Abigail stretched her shoulders and arms, waking up, but not yet wanting to leave the warm comfortable couch.

"How long was I asleep?"

"I don't know, half hour?" He watched as she rubbed her eyes and sat forward a little. "Do you want to go back to sleep?"

She shook her head 'no', "I'm fine." That 30 minutes had refreshed her completely and she was once again very aware of Jamie sitting so near her, looking homey and adorable.

"You're awake?" He asked.

"Yes, completely," she nodded.

His grin turned into a smile and his eyes twinkled with fun. "Want to see something cool?"

Chapter Ten

❦

The roof of The Thinking Bean was a flat industrial space. A huge square air conditioning unit covered in sheets of plastic tarp jutted up out of the roof near the back. Various pipes and vents stuck up in small groups at different degrees of height, billowing steam into the night. Weather beaten wood planks were built into a shoddy looking shed structure whose exact role was a mystery. A hip high brick wall bordered the edge of the entire roof, which discouraged anyone from stepping off and dropping to the sidewalk below. The top of the fire escape they had used to climb up was still visible on the other side of that brick wall from where they now stood, but just barely.

All of the charm and character of the old building that was present inside was non-existent on the roof. In fact, the roof of The Thinking Bean was one of the ugliest places Abigail had ever been. Still, she stood silently next to Jamie, enrapt with what he'd brought her to see.

Not the roof, but the view from the roof.

City Park stretched out over several blocks. The gazebo on the closest corner and the pond surrounded by trees on the far end, all sparkled with Christmas lights. The meandering pathways that ran throughout the park were lit by street lamps hung with shining Christmas wreaths. The two streets that lined the park opposite them were lit up in their own festive decorations. The windows of the little shops and restaurants along the streets were decorated by each owner, the street lamps on those streets were hung with wreaths and lights as well. A canopy of lights had been hung over Main Street, which was just past their view, but they could still see the canopy. Some of the more heavily decorated houses lit up the far distance.

From their vantage point, they could see every bit of Christmas joy on display all over Pitkin Point. It was breathtaking.

"This is amazing," she said.

He looked at her with one of his goofy smiles. "And that's not even the best part." Jamie took her by the elbow and turned her around so she was facing the old, crooked shed, "Stay there."

She watched and waited. Her feet were cold from being outside this long in her Elf shoes. It seemed like the temperature was even lower up here on the roof. But Jamie had draped one of his winter coats over her before they climbed out the window onto the fire escape and she snuggled comfortably into its spacious warmth now.

Jamie disappeared around the back of the dilapidated structure. She heard fumbling and a muffled curse word then, suddenly, the dark space he'd ducked into lit up. He stepped back into her view, backlit so she couldn't see his face, but she knew without a doubt that he wore a dorky smile.

"Ta-da!" He said, stretching his arm towards the light like a magician.

"What is it?"

"Come here," he reached a hand towards her and she went

to him, letting him take her hand and lead her around the corner.

What she found on the other side made her gasp with delight, "Oh, Jamie!"

Colored Christmas lights, the type with the big, round bulbs, were strung back and forth like a shining roof across a charming sitting space. A futon style outdoor seat with fat striped patio pillows placed along the back provided a comfortable place to sit. Two other patio chairs faced the large seat, each with their own all weather cushions, and a low iron table with a glass top served as a type of coffee table in the center. Everything rested on a deck that lifted the seating high enough to see over the roof wall. Positioned as near to the edge of the roof as possible while still being safe, with the shed acting as a wall on one side and, she guessed, a nice windbreak, the sitting area provided a wonderful view of the town below and the city beyond.

With the night sky above, the magical glow of the Christmas lights, and the stunning view, Abigail thought it might be one of the prettiest places she'd ever seen.

"Do you like it?" Jamie asked. He was watching her reaction.

"Like it?" Abigail stepped to the futon and sat down with a flourish, looking out across the Christmas-scape below them. "I love it!"

Jamie beamed, rocking back and forth on his heels like an excited kid.

"Come and sit." She patted the open space next to her.

Jamie tilted his head in her direction and took three quick strides that carried him to the low stairs, up the low stairs, past the chairs and to the futon seat in a matter of seconds. He turned his body and did a small jump like he was pole vaulting over an invisible barrier and landed heavily next to her. Abigail laughed.

"Did you build this?" She asked.

He nodded, "Yep."

"Does Zeke know it's here?"

He shook his head, "Nope."

She laughed again, "Really?"

He nodded. "Dillon and I built it right after I moved in here. I thought it would be good for us to have a place that was just ours, you know, father-son time."

"That's sweet," she said, and she meant it.

Jamie leaned back in the seat and put his feet up on the table, taking in the view. She did the same. The futon seat wasn't as wide as the couch inside, which meant their shoulders and arms were comfortably touching. Abigail didn't mind.

After a few minutes of quiet contemplation, Jamie turned to her, looking her up and down, her red and white striped tights and Elf shoes sticking out from underneath his giant winter coat.

"Are you warm enough?"

Abigail shrugged, "My feet are a little cold."

He sat up and she started to follow suit. But before she could, Jamie put his hand on her knee to stop her. "Stay here, I'll be right back."

He disappeared down the fire escape for a few minutes and she was alone on the roof. She listened to the occasional car driving past or sound of voices somewhere far below.

When Jamie returned, she heard him before she saw him. The metal rattling of the fire escape cut through the quiet around her and she watched as his head, backlit from the lights beyond, appeared at the edge of the building. He had carefully carried a bottle of wine in one hand with a wine opener already screwed partially into the cork as he made his way up the fire escape, which was really just a glorified ladder hanging on the outside of the building. He had a down sleeping bag hung over his shoulder and two wine glasses, one in each coat pocket.

Soon they were cuddled under the downy warmth of the sleeping bag. Jamie had unzipped it completely so it lay like a puffy square over them. He'd been sure to tuck the ends completely around her feet before snuggling in next to her and covering himself.

The warmth of the wine spread through her pretty quickly, seeing as she hadn't eaten any dinner. And the sleeping bag captured their body heat, making it nice and cozy for her Elf feet. Nice and cozy for her whole body.

They talked about a lot of things, and laughed about even more. Common memories of friends and family, of each other, growing up. By the time Jamie emptied the last of the wine into their glasses Abigail's sides hurt she'd laughed so hard.

"So, you really don't want to stay here?" Jamie asked, indicating Pitkin Point below with a nod of his head.

She shook her head a little too hard, the wine taking effect, "No!" Her voice carried far into the empty space around them.

"Why not?"

"I'm an artist, Jamie," she said it like he should already know the answer to his question. "Artists don't live in their tiny little home towns and marry their high school sweethearts and have babies," her words slurred a little as they came out, but the flow had already started and she couldn't stop it. "They go out into the big, bad world and make a name for themselves. They live in loft apartments and throw amazing parties. They don't cave to society. They stay up all night creating and scramble every month just to pay their electric bill and buy food. They meet brooding strangers and have anonymous sex..."

Jamie's eyebrows lifted. Abigail didn't know how to continue after that last comment, so she took a gulp of wine.

"Hmm, I didn't know that," he said, laughter in his eyes. He pretended to ponder the idea. "Is that what you've been doing since you moved away?"

She smacked his shoulder with her free hand and he exaggerated the power behind it, falling away from her in slow motion.

"Shut up," she giggled.

He sat up, pleased with himself as he took another drink of wine. After a few moments of calm, he continued the conversation.

"I guess I just don't understand. I mean, everybody's from somewhere. There's no shame in liking where you're from, even loving it. Is there?"

The words resonated with Abigail and she peered at him, taking in his roughed up hair, his kind, blue eyes, the squareness of his jaw, the shape of his mouth. Her gaze moved to the beautiful and, she had to admit, romantic little space he'd created here to look out over Pitkin Point. He appreciated the little things. That was nice. Whoever ended up with Jamie Turner would be a lucky woman.

The sound of metal rattling came to both of them at the same time and they looked first at the fire escape, then at each other, then back at the fire escape. The rattling got louder and before either of them could react, the silhouette of a head wearing a flat brimmed Deputy's hat appeared on the edge of the building.

"Charlie?" Jamie asked.

The figure kept climbing until its broad neck and shoulders appeared. It was breathing a little hard having just climbed up over two stories of fire escape ladder.

"Jamie is that you?" It was Charlie.

"Yeah, it's me," Jamie answered. He gave Abigail an

awkward glance before standing.

Charlie huffed and puffed his way over the top of the ladder and onto the roof. As soon as he got sure footing he turned on his high beamed flashlight and shone it on Jamie's face.

"Jeez, Charlie," Jamie lifted his hand to shield the blinding light.

The light switched to Abigail and she clenched her eyes closed against its brightness.

"Abigail?" Charlie asked.

"Yes, it's me," she answered, her eyes still squeezed shut.

"Stop shining that thing in our faces," Jamie said.

Abigail opened her eyes a peep and the light was no longer aimed at their faces.

"Are you guys drinking up here?" Charlie's voice conveyed that betrayal felt by an authority figure when they discover someone they like breaking the rules.

Abigail would have said 'no', except the light was shining directly on her hand holding her wine. She fought the sudden urge to laugh, and lost. Although, the laugh came out more like a snort.

"I brought the wine," Jamie volunteered.

"You can't have alcohol up here," Charlie informed them, all seriousness. Always seriousness.

"Are you kidding?" Jamie asked.

He wasn't.

Soon Abigail was climbing carefully down the fire escape using just one hand to hold on, while the other hand tried to keep her wine glass steady. She had insisted on taking her wine down with her. The glass was almost full after all. Charlie was below her on the fire escape and Jamie was above. It was slow going and, try as she may to steady it, the wine in her glass sloshed terribly, sometimes over the edges and down, she presumed, on top of Charlie's hat.

"Abby," Jamie said to her from somewhere above.

"Yeah?"

"Go into the apartment. I'll talk to Charlie," Jamie told her. She liked that he was going to manage this situation, because she was probably a little too tipsy to talk to Charlie with a straight face.

As she clambered into the apartment from the fire escape, a surprised Zeke and Fern watched her from where they sat on the couch.

"What are you doing?" Zeke asked.

"Coming in!" She said, laughing.

"Where's Jamie?"

"I think he might be getting a ticket," she answered, just as Jamie's figure climbed by the window on his way down to the ground.

Zeke stood up and came to the window, looking down at the alley below.

"Is that Charlie?" He asked. Abigail nodded then lifted her now half empty wine glass to Fern in greeting and took a sip.

"Were you on the roof?" Fern asked, obviously amused at the situation.

Abigail nodded.

"Charlie really is on a roll tonight," Zeke complained, still watching the two men in the alley.

"What do you mean?" Abigail asked, trying not to slur the phrase into 'whadya mean'.

"He gave me a ticket, too."

"What? Why?" Abigail was flabbergasted. "Were you drinking on the roof?"

"For noise pollution," Fern explained, rolling her sparkling blue eyes. She could even make an obnoxious teenager expression like the eye roll seem spunky and hip.

"Oh, wow," Abigail said. She thought about it for a few

more seconds then started giggling.

"It's not funny," Zeke said, turning from the window.

Abigail tried to contain her laughter, which only made it burst out more merrily.

Just then Jamie came through the door.

"That guy is too much," he said. His cheeks looked red, maybe from drinking wine or maybe from the exertion of climbing ladders and running up the stairs. But probably from getting a bogus ticket.

"Did he give you a ticket?" Zeke wanted to know.

"No, but he wanted to," Jamie answered. He looked at Abigail, who was still giggling in short little spurts. "I talked him out of it." He gave her a quick, reassuring wink, which was not lost on her brother.

Zeke switched his gaze to Abigail, who tried very hard to look serious. Then he looked at Jamie, then back to Abigail, "What were you guys doing up there?"

Jamie opened his mouth to say something, but Abigail beat him to it, "We were looking at the lights." Zeke's eyes dropped to the wine glass in her hand. She tipped it at him as if he held a glass and she was clinking his glass with hers. Then she said pointedly, "Relaxing."

Zeke didn't say anything, though she could tell he was itching to. He looked back and forth between her and Jamie again, then he looked to Fern. She held his gaze for a moment before expertly quieting his angst by tilting her head the tiniest bit and lifting one side of her mouth in a sweet smile.

Zeke closed his eyes, gathering his thoughts. When he opened them Abigail could tell he had decided not to get involved with whatever had happened, or was still happening, between her and Jamie.

"I hope you got all of your relaxing out of your system," Zeke stressed the word 'relaxing' with more than a little bit of sarcasm. "Because we have big plans for tomorrow."

Chapter Eleven

The following morning brought two big surprises.

First, the largest snowstorm the region had seen in a while was suddenly on the near horizon. The trajectory of an oncoming cold front had switched directions unexpectedly and Pitkin Point found itself in the path of a major winter wonderland producing storm one week before Christmas.

Second, parked outside The Thinking Bean was the next big event of Mistletoe Madness, a two horse team pulling a wagon full of hay or, as Zeke had dubbed it, The Jingle Bell Hay Ride.

The wooden wagon was charming, decked out with real pine boughs and big red bows draped along the sides. Inside the wagon were bales of hay set up like benches around the edges, so several people could sit and enjoy the slow moving scenery. Several thick horse blankets were thrown over the tops of the hay bales to make the seats more comfortable, and softer, plaid woolen blankets were folded in neat piles, ready to cover cold laps or shoulders if necessary.

A pair of white draft horses were hitched to the wagon,

their necks draped with brass sleigh bells and small red bows were tied into their flowing, white manes. A local rancher and friend of the family, Willard Gustaf, had brought the wagon and team for The Jingle Bell Hay Ride. In exchange for a small fee and a month's worth of free drinks at The Thinking Bean for himself and his wife, Emma, Willard would drive the team.

The Mistletoe Madness deal of the day was a free hay ride for anyone who purchased a drink in a to-go cup. Combine the availability of Santa Claus inside the coffee shop with the fact that it was the Saturday before Christmas and everyone was in town shopping anyway, made The Jingle Bell Hay Ride another huge success for Abigail's marketing genius big brother.

The place was packed and Abigail stayed busy all morning managing the ever growing line of little children who wanted to sit on Santa Claus' lap. She'd grown so accustomed to seeing Jamie in his Santa suit, as well as wearing her own costume, that she wondered what it would be like when they returned to wearing street clothes after Mistletoe Madness was over. In fact, she had started wondering what it would be like to find a job and move away after Christmas. Starting over once more in a faraway city. No longer seeing her parents and Zeke every day...or Jamie. Alone.

"Come on," Jamie said, reaching his hand towards her. She took it without knowing where they were going. She had been tucked into the farthest back corner of the book section, curled into one of the reading chairs that was shoved into a small nook there, sipping some hot tea and taking a little break. Jamie led her out towards the front of the store.

"Where are we going?" She asked.

He looked back at her, his smile hidden under the Santa beard, but visible in his eyes. "On a hay ride!"

Zeke had asked Jamie to go for a turn in the wagon and

wave like a friendly Santa at anyone and everyone he saw. Jamie told him he needed to take his Elf along. And now they were seated on one side of the wagon, sharing a hay bale and a blanket over their knees.

The day was definitely more cloudy and colder than it had been lately. The smell of snow was in the air and this seemed to have pulled more people into the main shopping streets of Pitkin Point. Christmas was almost here and snow was on the way. People needed to shop while the shopping was good.

The horse's hooves clopped on the pavement and their brass bells jingled merrily. A young family that Abigail didn't know sat opposite her and Jamie. The three little kids gawked at Jamie as he kept in character, ho-ho-ho-ing and waving at everyone they passed. Every now and then he would look sideways at one of the kids and give them a twinkly eyed smile or a wink.

The horses moved so slowly that it was possible to have conversations with people on the street as they passed. Abigail saw Judy outside Take the Cake and waved at her.

"Hi!" Judy exclaimed.

"Happy Holidays!" Abigail said.

Jamie gave Judy an official Santa Claus wave and she shook her head, laughing again.

"Your brother's got you guys hooked into his crazy stunts doesn't he?" She teased Abigail.

It was Abigail's turn to laugh, "He does!"

As the wagon inched away, Judy gestured towards her window and called out one more time to Abigail, "Everybody loves the window, by the way."

Abigail gave her a thumbs up.

"Dad!" A familiar voice came from further up the street. Jamie turned immediately and Abigail leaned out over the edge of the wagon past Jamie to see Dillon on the sidewalk in front of one of the town's best cafes. Raegan and Blake were with him. All three of them were watching the slow approach of Santa in the hay wagon with varying degrees of surprise on their faces.

Jamie beckoned Dillon over. "Come on, jump in!"

It warmed Abigail's heart to see the look on Dillon's face. Because teenagers are often stuck pretending to be grown up when, deep down, they still have a child's heart, she was afraid he was going to scowl and turn away. But instead, Dillon's face lit up at the chance to jump on the hay wagon, even if his Dad was dressed in a Santa Claus suit.

He started to run to the wagon then stopped at something Blake said. Dillon turned back to his mother and stepfather and Abigail held her breath. She could see Raegan talking, but couldn't hear them, of course. After a few tense moments, she saw Raegan dip her head in a reluctant 'yes' and Dillon ran to the wagon.

Dillon used one hand to grab the box of the wagon as Jamie took the other hand firmly in his. With a big lift and pull effort, Dillon was up over the side and sitting on a hay bale. The three little kids riding with them watched in awe as Santa Claus performed this stunt. Dillon, being a nice kid, didn't give away that Santa was his Dad during the whole ride.

"No reindeer today, Santa?" Dillon asked Jamie with a twinkle in his eyes that was familiar to Abigail. She'd seen it in Jamie's eyes a thousand times.

"Ho-ho-ho, not today little boy. The reindeers are resting, getting ready for Christmas Eve," Jamie answered, staying in character. He nudged Abigail with his elbow, "Isn't that right, Elf?"

"Yes, Santa, they need their rest," Abigail agreed.

Dillon grinned at her, still in a teasing mood, "Do you have a name, Elf?"

Abigail hesitated. Did she have an Elf name? She'd never

thought about it. She had just been Elf. Their three young passengers watched her with curiosity.

"Uh—sure, of course I do," Abigail said.

"Why, this is Abbah Dabbah Elf," Jamie chimed in, throwing in a ho-ho-ho for good measure.

"Abbah Dabbah Elf?" Dillon asked with playful skepticism.

"Yes, I'm Abbah Dabbah Elf," Abigail stuck her hand out to him as if they were meeting formally. Dillon took her hand and tipped an imaginary hat.

"Nice to meet you."

Somewhere along their route it started to snow. At first it was just a few flakes here and there that went unnoticed. But as the flakes became more regular they were tossed around on the chilling breeze that was picking up. The youngest of their fellow passengers, a little girl about three-years old, clapped her mittened hands together in front of her face and shouted, "It's snowing! It's snowing!"

Willard pulled the wagon up in front of The Thinking Bean a few minutes later. He climbed off of his seat at the front of the wagon and went to the back to help the young family get their little ones safely to the sidewalk. Jamie, Abigail and Dillon stood near the front end of the wagon box patiently waiting their turn. The great, white draft horse's ears flicked around, listening to all of the different sounds. Just as the last of the other family hopped to the ground, Zeke came out the front door to greet them.

As he stepped into the snow, he threw his arms up in his ringmaster move and declared, "It's snowing!"

Later, when they went over the details, they couldn't be sure why the horses spooked at the sight of Zeke's tall, spindly limbed Snowman costume, but spook they did.

The great beasts leaped in unison away from Zeke, heading sideways into the road with a clash of brass bells. As they forced the hitch into an unnatural position there was a horrible sound of crunching wood and metal added to the clamor of sleigh bells, and the horses bolted. Lurching forward, the wagon went out from under Abigail's feet and she started to tumble over the edge. Jamie grabbed her arm and pulled her back to the center of the wagon box where she sat down so hard her teeth smashed together.

Dillon, too, almost fell over the edge and was pulled back by his Dad. He fell on his hands and knees next to Abigail. The sound of men shouting faded away behind them as Jamie managed to grab hold of the front of the wagon box and stay on his feet. Because the reins were now dragging on the ground and whipping around the horse's back legs, they were even more spooked. The powerful draft horses were picking up speed and running away with the three of them stuck in back. Dillon started to get up.

"Stay down," Jamie shouted at him. He pulled his Santa hat, wig and beard off and dropped them into the wagon.

Dillon sat down next to Abigail. The horrible lurching and rumbling of the wagon rolled them back and forth and they bumped into each other repeatedly. She reached over and took his hand in hers, which he gripped tightly.

She could tell they were heading away from Main Street, which was good. With all of the people and cars out today a runaway team of horses would certainly cause chaos. Even though she was scared and being tossed around like a rag doll, Abigail tried to think about what they were approaching since they were heading away from Main Street. When the answer came, her stomach dropped with fear.

The train tracks.

She looked at Jamie as he was trying to keep his balance and they locked eyes. She knew that he knew exactly what she was thinking, because he was thinking it too.

It wasn't as if there were always trains on the train tracks, but there could be. Owen Jones had been killed crossing those train tracks when they were kids and Abigail had always been terrified of getting stuck on them. Jamie used to give her a hard time about her irrational fear of them.

"Do NOT get up," Jamie yelled at them again. Then he turned and started climbing up to the driver's seat.

Abigail didn't know if they were going faster than before, but it felt like they were. How long could horses run before they slowed down? What if they veered off the road or through a ditch? Wouldn't that roll the wagon? They could be thrown out, crushed, or trampled under the hooves of the huge draft horses.

Dillon looked at her, his eyes wide. She squeezed his hand and pulled him closer to her. She didn't want her fear to transfer to him. They both watched with growing panic as Jamie, the reins unreachable to him from the driver's seat, got ready to jump onto the horse's back.

With disbelief at what they were seeing, Abigail and Dillon sat mute and terrified in the back of the wagon. They watched as Jamie, looking like a young Santa surrounded by the swirling snowflakes of the oncoming storm, made a wild leap off of the driver's seat toward the broad backs of the draft horses. Without getting up, they couldn't see what happened after that. Abigail's heart was beating out of her chest. Where was Jamie? Why weren't they slowing down yet?

"Dad!" Dillon shouted, the same fear she had in her heart coming out in his voice.

"I've got 'em!" They heard Jamie's voice from somewhere on the other side of the driver's seat. Abigail thought she was going to cry she was so relieved. She did, actually, start to cry. She wrapped her arm around Dillon and they hugged in shared relief.

The horses began to slow down and within a few minutes

had stopped completely. A full quarter mile to the train track. The sound of a train whistle floated eerily through the light snow.

She and Dillon hopped off the back of the wagon as soon as it stopped. Abigail's knees wobbled a little as she landed on the ground and her stomach felt queasy.

"You okay?" Dillon asked her, a glimpse of the man he would eventually be coming through in his concern.

She nodded. "Yes, I'm fine."

They ran to the front of the wagon where Jamie was holding both of the horses gently by their bridles, talking low to them.

"Move slowly, they're still a little spooked," he said quietly. They did. As they approached, Jamie checked both of them with sideways glances, keeping most of his attention on the horses. "You both okay?"

"I think we're fine. What was that?" Abigail asked, trying to keep her voice calm.

"Yeah, Dad, what are you a stuntman or something?" Dillon added.

Jamie chuckled.

A few minutes later they were surrounded by people. Some had ran after them, some had driven their cars. Willard got there and took over caring for the horses. Deputy Diego pulled up in the sheriff's car. Abigail said a little prayer of thanks that Charlie wasn't on duty today. He would have probably locked them all up for several violations under obscure runaway horse laws.

Jamie looked after Dillon until Raegan showed up in a flurry of concern. Before leaving with her, Dillon gave his Dad a bear hug. Then he turned to Abigail and gave her one, too.

"Thank you, Dillon," she said.

"Thank you, Abby," he said and a little piece of her heart melted.

"See ya, Stuntman Santa." Dillon pointed at Jamie as he walked backwards towards his mother. Jamie waved his comment off, but Abigail could tell it meant something to him that his teenage son obviously thought he was cool.

Zeke showed up, stripped of his Snowman costume, wearing a pair of jeans he'd hastily pulled over his black leggings.

"Holy cow!" He said as he walked up to them both and grabbed them in his long, lanky arms. "Are you all right? Where's Dillon?"

"He's fine," Jamie said.

"We're fine," Abigail said. As she did her arm slipped easily around Jamie's waist in a show of solidarity. He grinned at her and put his arm, still wrapped in his Santa suit, around her shoulders.

"What are you doin' Snowman? Scaring the horses!" Jamie pushed Zeke's shoulder in jest.

"I am so sorry," Zeke said. His long face was full of guilt. Mistletoe Madness had gotten away from him and he knew it. "We're trimming the tree at Mom and Dad's tonight. Having dinner and eggnog and such. You and Dillon should come. My Mom is worried sick about you both," Zeke said.

Jamie looked at Abigail. "Is it okay with you if we come over?"

She nodded. Yes, that was perfectly okay with her.

Chapter Twelve

Zeke sent Abigail and Jamie home after their ordeal. Willard hauled the overly excited draft horses back to his place and Fern stepped in to help Zeke out for the rest of the afternoon at The Thinking Bean.

Even though she went straight home and didn't think she'd been too affected, Abigail couldn't shake the shivering sensation in her stomach. Adrenaline, she guessed.

Her Mom insisted that she take a hot bath right away, which she did. She put on some fuzzy fleece pants and a sweater while her hair dried into its curly mop. Her Mom was in the kitchen cooking goodies for their evening party, but she wouldn't hear of Abigail helping her or exerting herself in any way.

"You've been through a shocking experience, sweetie. You need to rest," she told her daughter.

Her Dad was in the living room going through lights for the tree. Abigail sat with him, sipping hot tea and watching the snow as it continued to fall outside.

Phantoms of the event came upon her every few minutes. The jolt of the wagon under her feet when it almost threw her out. Jamie's hand yanking her to safety. The look on Dillon's face as Jamie climbed up onto the driver's seat. The terrifying moment Jamie leaped out of their sight and they didn't know if he had made it or fallen under the wagon.

As the hours ticked away she began to wonder if the shiver in her stomach had to do completely with the runaway wagon or if it was also because Jamie was coming over. The thought of seeing him again kept slipping into her mind and filling her whole body with a fluttering anticipation. Distracted by the feeling, she had to ask her Dad to repeat himself whenever he said anything.

"Are you feeling okay, Abigail?" He finally asked. He was sitting in his corner chair, piles of tangled Christmas lights in his lap as well as to his right and left on the floor. His sharp eyes looked at her over the top of his glasses.

"I'm just a little shaky," she answered.

"Because of the wagon incident?"

She shrugged, taking a sip of her tea. Her fingers trembled on the warm mug. Her father watched her evenly over his glasses. His psychology brain patiently waiting for the truth to come to the surface.

"Is that all that's bothering you?" He asked.

Well, maybe not 100% patient.

"What else would it be?" She deflected.

He leaned back in his chair, "Well, now, let me see. You did recently lose your job, you packed up and left your apartment and the life you'd built and came home..." Again he peered over his glasses.

"Oh, that," she said.

"Yes, that."

She shrugged again.

"And there's Jamie," he said.

Abigail's stomach did a flip flop, "What? What about Jamie?"

"Your mother told me there's some possibility of a...a bit of a romance between you two?"

"She said what?"

He seemed surprised at her surprise. "Is she wrong?"

"What? No! I don't know!" Abigail was flustered.

"Any one of these situations can cause feelings of uncertainty or anxiety. Although, as your father, I would hope that a romance would make you happy, not anxious."

"There's no romance, Dad," Abigail said.

Her father seemed disappointed. "That's too bad, I've always liked Jamie."

She paused, curiosity overcoming exasperation. "You have?"

"Yes," he nodded slowly as he spoke. "He was a good friend to Zeke, and you. A nice, steady character, even when he was young." Again he peered over his glasses at her, this time with a smile in his eyes. "He doted over you when you were kids, that's for sure. A father likes a young man who dotes over his daughter."

"He did not dote over me." She waved her hand in the air as if erasing what her Dad had just said. Even as her stomach burst into butterflies.

"Well, you never wanted him to, but he did. It was painful to watch sometimes."

"Dad, stop."

He smiled at her, "Okay, okay, no more talk about romance."

He was true to his word and didn't say anything more about Jamie, but that didn't mean Abigail wasn't thinking about him. She excused herself to her room to get ready and spent the next few hours agonizing over what to wear for the tree trimming. Then chastising herself for fretting. She didn't want to look shaky or uncertain about anything. She also didn't want to look too fixed up, like she was trying too hard.

Yet, she did want Jamie to like what she wore. She liked the way his eyes lit up when he saw her dressed up. Then she felt guilty and ridiculous for feeling that way.

She was completely out of sorts about all of it.

Finally, she decided on a pair of jeans, a simple off-white V-neck sweater with flared sleeves and a pearl pendant necklace.

When she was finally ready, she took a long look in the mirror. Her jeans were her most flattering pair, the sweater was soft and hung nicely over her curves, her hair had extra shine and bounce because she'd let it air dry all afternoon. Abigail determined she looked fine, as good as she was going to look at least. It's not like this was a date or anything.

She went upstairs and found Zeke and Fern already arrived. Fern was becoming a regular fixture in Zeke's world. Their parents, Mom especially, couldn't have been more thrilled.

Abigail made conversation with Fern over the spinach dip, although she didn't eat any. Her stomach still felt fluttery.

The snow was really coming down now. What if Jamie decided not to come, choosing instead to ride out the storm and spend some quality time with Dillon on his own at the empty apartment? An irrational glumness fell over her. Zeke offered her some eggnog and she refused.

A firm knock on the door lifted her spirits and she almost ran to answer it. Managing to keep her cool, Abigail moved towards the door, but Zeke got to it first.

"There they are!" Zeke exclaimed.

And there they were. Jamie and Dillon came in the front door, brushing snow off their shoulders and stamping it from their boots. They both looked taller in her parent's house. Jamie especially.

"Thanks for inviting us," Jamie said as their Dad came to greet them.

"It's the least we could do after Zeke tried to kill you!"

Everyone laughed. Zeke groaned and took their coats to hang up. Jamie pulled his hat off, handing it to Zeke, leaving his hair in its signature out of control style. He ran one hand through it in an attempt to tame it and that's when he saw her. He paused, their eyes locking from across the room and everyone else fell away into the background. The fluttering in her stomach expanded and reached her heart, making it skip a beat. Even from across the room she could see the glimmer in his eyes.

Jamie's hand dropped and he smoothed the fabric of his black dress shirt. She couldn't look away from him. The side of his mouth lifted into a crooked, sexy smile.

"Jamie!" Her mother crowded past the others and gave him a hug. Then she turned to Dillon. "Dillon, Merry Christmas!" She hugged him, too. This kicked off a hugging fiesta between all of them, peppered with holiday greetings. Jamie hugged his way to her. First her Mom, then her Dad, then Fern, then he stood in front of Abigail, looking down at her, his body pressed against hers in the crowded, small space.

"Merry Christmas, Abby," he said softly, and wrapped his arms around her waist, pulling her into him for a hug. She let her arms circle his neck, pressing her cheek against his. His face was still a little cold from being outside, but his body was warm and strong, and he smelled amazing.

"Merry Christmas, Jamie," she whispered into his ear. His arms tightened around her, making her heart beat even faster. For a few moments Abigail was utterly lost in his embrace. She didn't want him to let go.

But let go he must. There was dinner to serve and eggnog to drink and, of course, a tree that needed trimming.

They had prime rib, which was delicious, and garlic mashed potatoes, and a wilted salad made with greens, bacon and a hot dressing. Abigail, Jamie and Dillon sat on one side of the long dining room table. Zeke and Fern sat on the other. Mom and Dad sat on each end.

Abigail was glad to be sitting next to Jamie. She knew she was having exaggerated feelings because of their earlier ordeal, but she felt safe next to him. It was a nice feeling, especially when her parents asked for details of the runaway wagon.

Dillon chimed in and told the story of how Jamie, in full Santa regalia, saved the day. It was good to hear him so animated and open. He told the story with a lot of funny details that made all of them laugh.

"How did you know what to do?" Her father asked Jamie.

Jamie shrugged. "I've seen a lot of westerns."

"You're crazy," Zeke said, laughing into his wine glass before taking a sip.

Abigail laughed along with everyone else, but she felt the shivering in her stomach again and she had to press her hands into her lap to hide the fact that they were trembling.

Jamie noticed and gave her a quiet, questioning look. She smiled weakly at him then had to look at her plate. She wasn't trying to make a scene. She felt queasy and wished she hadn't eaten so much dinner.

Jamie continued talking and laughing with Zeke and her parents, while at the same time reaching under the tablecloth and finding her hands clenched in her lap, ice cold. He wrapped his hand over hers, holding them, comforting her quietly. His touch calmed her stomach and she glanced at him. He didn't look at her, but gave her hands a squeeze under the table, telling her everything was all right while never letting on to anyone else.

After dinner they all moved into the living room to trim the tree. With her parents taking on the role of surrogate grandma and grandpa to Dillon, Zeke and Fern making eyes at each other over the eggnog, and she and Jamie sewing long strings of popcorn and cranberries together on the couch, the whole scene had a very hometown family Christmas vibe. Abigail was enjoying it more than she ever thought possible.

"How do you do this?" Jamie asked her. His thick fingers weren't conducive to the fine work of pushing a needle through the fat end of a piece of popcorn with a light enough touch that it didn't break. He had shattered several pieces already.

Abigail giggled, "Here." She handed him her string that already had three pieces of popcorn strung in a row. "Let's trade. You do my cranberries and I'll do your popcorn."

"Thank you." He carefully picked a cranberry out of the bowl and pushed his needle through it lengthwise. He lowered his voice conspiratorially, "I don't want your Mom to think I'm shirking my duties."

Abigail glanced at her mother, who was in the middle of offering Dillon another cookie from a mound of Christmas cookies she had balanced on a platter.

"I think she's distracted trying to put your son into a sugar coma," Abigail said.

Jamie laughed. There were his dimples, and the corners of his eyes crinkling up, lifting her into a state of delight. She had a sudden urge to lean over and kiss him on the cheek. The idea startled her so much she stopped sewing and stared at him.

"What?" Jamie asked, noticing her focused attention. "Am I doing it wrong?" He held up his neatly sewn cranberries for inspection.

"No," Abigail said. She blinked, but didn't look away, "You're doing everything right."

Say what she would about Jamie Turner, that he was goofy and joked too much and had infuriated her all through her formative teenage years, but the man knew when a woman was thinking about kissing him. That was obvious.

His expression changed. He looked deeply into her eyes, allowing his gaze to slide down her cheek and across her lips before lifting it again. When he spoke, his voice was gruff, a bedroom voice if she'd ever heard one, "Abby..."

A crackling sensation shuddered through her. As if she'd touched a live wire. But she hadn't touched anything. Only on the truth. She wanted Jamie. She could see them being together. She trusted him. And, most earth shattering of all, she loved him.

Abigail swallowed hard. Chills shot up and down her spine then across her shoulders and down her arms, making her shiver.

"Abby, I-" he started.

"Take me to the Christmas dance," Abigail interrupted him. She pressed her knee into his, leaning towards him, wishing he could take her in his arms right now.

Abigail had never felt like this before, so certain she was right, so absolutely convinced that everything she'd ever wanted had been staring her in the face her entire life. She'd finally seen it.

"Take you to the dance?" He looked disoriented. He hadn't expected that.

She nodded with such conviction her curls bounced. "I want to go to the Christmas dance with you."

A smile slowly took over his face and when it was complete, Jamie was beaming. She basked in his happiness. As sure of his feelings as she was her own.

"That's a great idea. I kinda wanted to bring that up myself, but I didn't know if you'd be open to it," he said. "It will be nice to go with a friend. No pressure, you know?"

Chapter Thirteen

The winter storm hit in full force on the same day as The Dickens Party. That was the day before Christmas Eve, and it rang in with almost three feet of snow, white out driving conditions, and winds that reached blizzard force. Most people had the good sense to stay inside. Batten down the hatches and spend the day cooking or reading or sitting by a nice, cozy fire.

Zeke was not most people.

His dedication to the Mistletoe Madness schedule was real. Insisting that they continue with their plans for the day, he bickered with Abigail over the phone about when she was planning on coming in and what she was going to wear.

"Zeke, I'm not driving in this weather and, if I was, I would not wear that stupid Elf costume," she told him from the living room couch.

"Of course you're not wearing the Elf costume. It's the Dickens Party today. Don't worry, Fern has some extra things you can wear for this party," he said.

Why wasn't she surprised that Fern had a variety of Victorian era clothes laying around? Probably steampunk.

"Zeke, I–"

"Jamie's coming to get you so you don't have to drive," her brother said.

That was not what she wanted to hear.

"No, Zeke, that's ridiculous. Tell him not to do that," she insisted.

The last thing she wanted was to be alone with Jamie for any reason. It was humiliating enough that she'd asked him to the dance when it turned out he had no feelings for her whatsoever. On top of that she couldn't come up with a good reason to get out of it. She really, really didn't want to ride with him through a blizzard to work at The Thinking Bean.

"Too late, he already left," Zeke informed her.

Sure enough, a few minutes later there was a knock on the front door. She let her Dad answer, wanting to avoid looking Jamie in the eye for as long as possible. He'd come out in a blizzard to get her, she could hardly tell him to go away.

As he chatted with her Dad about the condition of the roads, Abigail pulled on her heaviest coat, her snow boots, and a red wool hat. Then she wrapped a long red wool scarf several times around her neck and up over her mouth. Partly to protect herself from the cold and partly to keep her emotions masked.

Outside, the wind blew the snow hard into her face as she followed Jamie down the sidewalk. His old pickup that he used to do odd handyman jobs was running and warm, waiting for them. When they got closer to the street and away from the protection of the house, Jamie took her arm in a firm grip and walked her to the passenger side of the pickup. The protective move made her heart sad.

Inside the cab Christmas music blasted along with the heater. Jamie turned the volume down.

"Nothing like a ton of snow to get you in the Christmas spirit," he said, putting on his seatbelt.

Abigail nodded, pretending that she was too cold to uncover her mouth. Maybe she could make the whole ride without any real conversation. It was only a five minute drive to The Thinking Bean from her parent's house. She failed to calculate the additional time it would take to drive through blinding snow flurries, contend with ice building up on the windshield, and huge drifts of snow blocking some of the main roads.

"We'll get there, I promise," Jamie told her at one point.

She believed him, but she remained quiet. This whole thing seemed like an exercise in futility. The Dickens Party, The Thinking Bean, the Christmas Dance, all of it was just a huge waste of time. Nobody was coming out in this kind of weather to go to a coffee shop party. She and Jamie were going to the dance as friends only. She had misread everything and he didn't have romantic feelings for her after all. Yet her feelings had only now become clear and they were making her miserable.

She was in the impossibly ridiculous situation of being in love with Jamie Turner and crushed under the realization that he didn't love her back. Probably never had.

They pulled up to The Thinking Bean, which was just a blur of bricks behind a wall of blowing snow this morning. As soon as Jamie put the pickup in park, Abigail hopped out of her side and headed straight for where she thought the door was located. Certainly she could find her way across a sidewalk in a blizzard without his help. The less she could interact with Jamie today, the better.

As expected, the shop was empty save for Zeke and Fern. The smell of fresh coffee greeted her as she pushed through the door, followed by Jamie and a harsh gust of wind carrying wet, heavy snow.

"Yuletide Greetings, sister!" Zeke called out to her. He

was decked out in a white dress shirt, red paisley vest and, of course, his now infamous top hat.

She pulled the scarf from her face and glared at him, "Bah humbug."

"Come with me." Fern helped her out of her coat. "I have some adorable things you can wear."

Without a backwards glance, Abigail followed Fern upstairs to choose from several high waisted, floor length, flouncing skirts and fitted jackets hung up in Zeke's bedroom. They were definitely steampunk, but still very doable for a modern day Dickens party.

Abigail chose a skirt in a broad red and black plaid and a black jacket that buttoned tightly around her waist and flounced out over her hips and bottom. Fern wore a black and tan striped skirt in a similar cut and a brown V-neck jacket that also had a high collar with stiff ruffles along the edge, which showed off her elegant neck and pixie blonde hair cut.

"Thank you, Fern," Abigail said, twirling in a circle. "You have beautiful clothes."

"You look gorgeous in that, especially with your hair," Fern gushed. She gave Abigail a knowing look, "Jamie is going to trip over himself when he sees you."

The words shot through Abigail's injured ego and pierced her aching heart. All of the color drained out of her face, making her even more pale than normal.

"Are you okay?" Fern asked.

Abigail couldn't answer without crying. And she absolutely did not want to cry. She avoided looking Fern in the eye and sat down on the edge of Zeke's bed, biting her lower lip.

"Abigail, what's the matter?" Fern, full of concern, sat down next to her and Abigail couldn't hold it all in anymore. She spilled the beans.

She told Fern about her and Jamie's lifelong relationship, growing up together, the wonderful times, the misunderstandings. She told her about how she'd been attracted to him ever since returning and that she'd thought he felt the same way. As she relayed the moment she realized that she was in love with him and asked him to the dance, then what he'd said in return, Abigail teared up. Her heart was hurting knowing that Jamie just wanted to be friends, but it did feel good to tell someone else the whole story.

"Oh, honey." Fern patted Abigail's back, her brow furrowed with dismay. "That's terrible." As she patted her back, Fern's dismay turned into something else. Confusion.

"What is it?" Abigail sniffed.

"It's just...I don't understand. I thought he was really into you. I mean, he can barely take his eyes off you," Fern explained. "It just doesn't make sense."

"I don't know," Abigail sighed and sniffed again.

"Maybe he's one of those weirdos that only likes you until you like them back," Fern suggested. They both chuckled at the idea.

"He is kind of weird, I guess," Abigail said. They laughed again. Somehow, this little heart-to-heart made her feel better.

By the time they went back downstairs she was able to face the situation with some grace. The stylish steampunk outfit helped.

There was still nobody in the shop. Zeke sat on the couch in the cafe area, sipping a Cappuccino. Jamie wasn't anywhere around.

"Where's Jamie?" Fern asked, glancing at Abigail.

"He won't button his vest so he is not allowed in the front where customers might see him," Zeke spoke extra loud so anyone on the first floor could hear him.

Jamie's frustrated voice came from the storage room, "I'll button the vest when another human being shows up!"

"He's pouting," Zeke told them. Fern raised her eyebrows at Abigail and they joined Zeke.

They played a game of cards to pass the time. Outside the wall to ceiling windows the snow continued to come down hard. Another foot or more of fresh snow built up on Jamie's pickup, and he still hadn't emerged into the cafe area.

Abigail excused herself to go look for a book to read to pass the time. That's when she found him. He was sitting in one of the chairs up against the window in the front book section. A pile of botany books balanced on the spindly table next to him, the lamp gave off a warm glow.

Jamie had on dark jeans and boots, a white dress shirt and a forest green vest, unbuttoned. He looked up when she walked towards him and she felt the familiar thrill move through her body when she caught his eye. She smiled at him because she couldn't help herself. He moved like he was going to stand.

"Don't get up," she said. She moved gracefully towards him, enjoying the swishing of the elaborate skirt and knowing that, if nothing else, she looked quite eye catching in her ensemble. She sat down in the other chair nestled next to his.

"You look great." He hadn't looked away from her the entire time.

She thought about what Fern had said, that Jamie couldn't take his eyes off of her. She smiled quietly at him. Not sure what to think about any of it anymore.

"Thank you, you look nice, too."

Jamie's face turned a little red and Abigail had a glimmer of hope flit across her heart. She picked up one of the books in his stack.

"Urban Botanics?" She raised an eyebrow.

The sound of the front door opening and new voices chattering interrupted them. A cold draft of air came around the corner.

"Customers!" Zeke called out so Jamie, so the whole world, could hear. Jamie lifted his gaze to the ceiling and stood up, buttoning his vest.

He offered her his hand, "My lady?"

She took his hand.

The Dickens Party had officially begun.

※

ONCE ABIGAIL TOLD her mother that she was going to the Christmas Dance with Jamie, Sarah Ackerman went a little bonkers. Offering multiple suggestions of what she could possibly wear, only to refute each suggestion with a mumbled comment, "No, that's too casual...Too risqué, that won't do...The material is too thin, she'll freeze to death!"

"Mom, it doesn't matter. I'll just wear my black skirt," Abigail suggested.

"Oh, sweetie, you don't want to look like an old lady, do you?"

Quite honestly, Abigail had lost her enthusiasm for going to the dance the moment Jamie assumed they were going as friends. It didn't really matter what she wore. The chance of the evening turning into a romantic date were next to nil. And the weather made it impossible for them to drive to the city and go shopping for anything spectacular anyway. If she had her way the dance would disappear in a puff of smoke and she wouldn't have to think about it anymore.

For a brief time during The Dickens Party Abigail thought maybe her wish would come true. Deputy Diego had stopped by to make sure they were all right and let it slip that the town council might cancel the dance due to the weather. But that did not happen. The snow had stopped before nightfall and any rumors of Pitkin Point giving in to Mother Nature were squelched. They would dig out and persevere.

The Christmas Dance would proceed on Christmas Eve the way it had for over 50 years. Abigail was doomed to go and have her heart crushed.

"Sweetie." A knock sounded on her bedroom door. Her Mom opened the door and poked her head in. "Can I show you something?"

Abigail was relaxing in her bedroom, trying to decide if she should start looking for jobs online now or wait until the holidays were over.

"Sure, Mom, come in," she sat up and threw her legs off the bed so she was sitting on the edge.

"Look what I found!" Her Mom stepped into the room carrying a long, midnight blue dress on a hanger.

It was the dress she'd worn to the Christmas Dance in high school. The one Jamie had told her he remembered.

"Where did you find that?" Abigail stood and inspected the dress. It was still beautiful, deep blue velvet, a scalloped neckline, crystals sewn into the bodice, along the cuffs of the long sleeves, and on the hem.

"It was hanging in the closet of my sewing room...your old room." Her mother was beaming. "I think you should wear this to the dance," she said, unable to contain her excitement.

"This?" Abigail eyed the garment again. "It's so old, isn't it?"

"Oh, this kind of dress never goes out of style."

"I don't think it would fit me anymore."

"I can take it out if you need me to. It's such a beautiful color on you, Abigail. And the material, look at the material. So rich."

The dress was exquisite. She remembered feeling like a princess in that dress. Like the most beautiful girl in town. It had been the dress that inspired Jamie to ask her to prom. Was it pathetic of her to wear it now? Would he think she was trying to drum up old feelings, trick him into liking her again?

"Try it on." Her Mom pulled the dress off of its hanger.

After a moment's hesitation, Abigail thought why not?

A few small areas would need adjusting, Abigail was a bit curvier now than she had been in high school, but otherwise the dress fit. Not only that, her Mom had a long, white winter cloak and a matching white winter hat and gloves that she convinced Abigail would go perfectly with the dress. Abigail had a pair of knee high white boots to complete the look.

She had the perfect dress to wear to the dance, and she was in love with her date. Still, Abigail wished with all of her heart that she didn't have to go.

Chapter Fourteen

On the morning of Christmas Eve every person in Pitkin Point who owned a snow blower or a plow on the front of their pickup, or a hand held heavy duty snow shovel, chipped in to dig out the park. With so many hands the job of clearing the pathways, the gazebo, and the open areas where the dance floor was later laid out, was short work. Despite the bitter cold, everyone was excited. The snow that covered everything as far as the eye could see, combined with the already placed lights and decorations, made this one of the most magical backgrounds any of them had ever seen for the Christmas Dance.

Jamie was one of the people working on snow removal, so Abigail didn't see or talk to him all day on Christmas Eve. Maybe he would be too tired to go to the dance at all, she ventured to hope.

No luck there. Jamie called at 6:00 to double check that he would be picking her up at 7:00.

"Yes, that's fine," she said.

"Wait till you see it, Abby," he said with delight. "It's

really something else. You know that song 'Winter Wonderland'?"

"Yes."

"That's exactly what it looks like."

When the call ended, sadness welled up in her again and she had to let it out. A good cry into her pillow while face down on her bed helped...a little. She washed her face and did her makeup, got dressed in the blue dress that now fit perfectly thanks to her Mom, and gathered her pure white cloak, hat, and fuzzy gloves. With nothing else to do but wait, she sat down on the living room couch and looked at the Christmas tree, trying to get into the spirit of the evening.

Not even Jamie's obvious pleasure at seeing her did anything to lift her mood.

"Wow," he finally spoke after an extended pause where he simply gazed at her after being shown in the door by her Dad.

Abigail shifted uncomfortably from one foot to the other. She had originally wanted him to think she looked pretty, but she felt no joy in it now. It didn't change anything else about their relationship. A dark cloud hung over her tonight and nothing was getting through.

Jamie tilted his head and looked harder at the front of her dress where it showed through the opening of her cloak.

"Is that...is that your old blue dress?" He asked.

Abigail felt heat rising in her cheeks. What a way to start the evening.

"Mom altered it. I only wore it once," she defended herself.

"No, I didn't mean it like that. I like that dress," he said.

She flounced by him, not wanting to talk about it.

"Ready to go?" She asked.

Jamie was surprised at her reaction. He looked with confusion at her parents, who were seeing them off before getting themselves out the door and to the dance. Her Dad patted him on the shoulder in a show of solidarity or support or condolence, it wasn't clear which.

Abigail was prepared for many disappointments this evening. Jamie's description of the beautiful landscape surrounding the cleared area of the dance was not one of them. All of the extra snow did make it look enchanting, like they were going to a dance inside of a giant Christmas snow globe.

Jamie offered her his arm and watched her reaction as they entered the park, "What do you think?"

"It's just stunning," she said. Not only were they surrounded by undulating drifts of snow on all sides, but the snow had blanketed the trees, gazebo, streetlamp and wreaths as well. The Christmas decorations twinkled and winked through the frozen white.

There was a bonfire in the center of the park and gas patio heaters that looked like small fire pits were placed strategically near benches, the dance floor, and the band, keeping everyone warm. There were booths set up where you could get roasted chestnuts, hot chocolate or hot apple cider, and fresh kettle corn that was made right there in a huge cast iron kettle heating on its own fire.

What made Abigail's spirits lift most of all, however, were the people. The whole town of Pitkin Point had come out dressed in their warmest and finest clothes. They had brought the Christmas spirit with them and were talking, laughing and dancing. The feeling of celebration was everywhere and Abigail realized that she wouldn't be able to stay in her dark mood while in this place.

"You make it even more beautiful," Jamie said. His voice brought her attention back to him, to them, standing arm-in-arm at the edge of the Christmas Dance. He was gazing at her, something of a dreamy look in his eyes.

She started to say something when she was distracted by a

top hat peeking out from a group of people nearby. The top hat moved swiftly towards them.

"Merry Christmas!" Zeke greeted them happily. His black overcoat and bright green scarf wrapped several times around his neck went well with the top hat. He was grinning ear to ear and Abigail knew why. Fern was on his arm.

"Abigail," Fern exclaimed, "You look like a snow princess!"

Abigail blushed at the compliment, especially coming from Fern who looked amazing in one of her steampunk style skirts in green plaid and a Victorian style wool coat that showed off her figure.

"That's exactly what she looks like, a snow princess," Jamie agreed.

Fern's eyebrows lifted and she gave Abigail a look. The band started a new song, a waltz. Jamie turned to face Abigail and bowed. She had been so distracted with her dark mood and wanting to avoid the dance in general that she'd barely looked at him or what he was wearing...until now.

If she had to choose one word to describe Jamie's attire this evening, that word would be 'dashing'.

He wore a heavy black coat with a wide collar that was turned up against the cold. Two rows of brass buttons ran from just under the collar to his waist, pulling the coat in tight and warm, and emphasizing his masculine form. His hair was not quite as wild as it had a tendency to get, contained and shaped with some product and effort on his part, but still a rich, wavy brown. He wore a blue wool scarf knotted and tucked into the front of his coat. She hadn't noticed the scarf before, it was the same midnight blue of her dress.

He looked mature and handsome. Quietly watching her reaction. Patiently waiting for her to take notice of him. Like always.

She felt the blush on her cheek turn into something more, that impossible sparkling smile that happens when love cannot hide any longer. She couldn't help herself, even if he didn't feel the same way. Looking at Jamie Turner in this winter wonderland, the music floating around them, the lights twinkling behind him, she loved him more than ever.

"Thank you," she said.

Jamie's face broke into his crooked, goofy smile. The smile he'd given her the very first time they met in grade school. The smile she'd seen thousands of times. Countless times. The smile she now knew had lived deep in her heart her whole life.

"Would you like to dance?" He asked, offering her his black leather gloved hand.

She nodded and placed her soft, white gloved hand in his. He gripped it carefully and led her to the middle of the dance floor where he twirled her once under his arm before placing one hand on her waist and one holding her hand in proper waltz stance. She laughed with surprise at his expertise as she placed her free hand on his shoulder.

"You waltz?" She asked.

He nodded, "I learned after the last time I saw you in that dress."

With that confession Jamie Turner took her breath away. He moved her smoothly across the dance floor, turning slowly, using the lightest pressure of his hand in hers or on her waist to lead. She couldn't take her eyes off of him. She could barely breathe. They were no longer dancing, they had been lifted into the air and were floating. The cold fell away, the other dancers fell away, only the music and Jamie were here on this starry Christmas Eve.

It was truly starry, too. The storm had officially moved on and left in its wake a blanket of twinkling stars that glimmered over everyone at the Christmas Dance. But none more than Abigail and Jamie.

They danced until the band took a break and they were forced to mingle with mere mortals again. Jamie got them both hot apple cider and they strolled to the frozen pond and back. A section of the pond had been roped off and ice skaters, mostly kids and families with small children, skimmed across the top. As they walked, friends and acquaintances greeted them, everyone smiling and waving, sometimes congratulating them for surviving the runaway wagon incident. Always merry, always kind.

One such interaction was with Frank Adams, the owner of the local bowling alley and bar.

"Merry Christmas, you two," Frank said. His barrel chest even larger than normal because it was wrapped in layers for warmth.

"Merry Christmas, Frank," Jamie said.

"Merry Christmas," Abigail echoed.

"Say, I saw your work at the coffee shop, and at Judy's place," Frank said to Abigail. Her work? He must mean the window paintings. "I was wondering if I could hire you to do something like that for my place?"

"Window painting?" Abigail clarified.

"Yes, not Christmas, of course, since it's almost over. But for New Year's Eve. We're having a big party that night," Frank explained.

Abby nodded, pleased at the idea. "Sure, Frank. I'll come by the day after Christmas."

With that settled, she and Jamie continued on their stroll back, she hoped, to the dance floor. As they walked an idea popped into her head and distracted her from their surroundings.

After a minute, Jamie noticed. "What are you thinking about so hard?"

She came back to the dance, to him. "Oh, nothing really."

"It looks like more than nothing," he pressed.

"I was just thinking...I wonder how many other businesses might want their windows painted?"

Jamie raised his eyebrows, impressed at the idea, nodding in agreement, "And they could hire someone like you to paint them?"

"Yes, something like that," she said. Her mind clicked along, trying to quickly calculate how much work that would mean for someone who was needing to find a job.

Another minute passed in silence as they got closer and closer to the dance floor. Jamie cleared his throat.

"So you're thinking you might stay here? Start a business?" He asked.

His question lacked emotion, but Abigail's response was strong anyway. A sense of possibility filled her heart. Perhaps she could run her own business, paint for a living, not have to leave her family, her friends, or Jamie.

She looked at him sideways as they walked. Her arm was still linked in his. It felt right for them to be a couple at the Christmas Dance. She wondered if any of this mattered to him as much as it mattered to her.

"I think I would consider it, for sure. If I could build up a freelance kind of business and paint my own artwork on the side."

"You think you would be happy living a small town life?"

She looked around at the glittering snow covered dance and leaned into his arm, smiling, "It's growing on me."

They were at the gazebo, a few couples stood inside looking out over the park. Jamie stopped and turned to her. "Want to go in the gazebo?"

The musicians were warming up, back from their break. Abigail looked towards them, wanting to float again.

"You don't want to dance?" She asked him.

Jamie glanced at the dance floor that was beginning to fill with people. He looked back at her, into her eyes, excited about something, that much she could tell. "In a minute. Let's go up here first."

He took her hand and led her up the stairs. Back to the exact place they'd stood only days ago. The day they'd decided to just be friends.

A little of the magic drained out of Abigail as they stood there. The view was still beautiful, even more so tonight than it had been on that night. But the memory of that conversation made her sad. It made tonight seem like nothing more than wishful thinking on her part. A fantasy that would disappear like Cinderella's dress and carriage at midnight.

The other couples left the gazebo. Called by the music back to the dance floor. Yet she and Jamie stayed, like silent statues watching happiness pass in front of them, not being able to reach out and take some of their own.

Jamie started talking, his eyes still trained on the couples dancing. "It's been quite a Christmas, hasn't it?"

"Yes, it has," she answered. Miserable at the idea of their date being reduced to small talk.

"It's been good, though, working with you and...everything," he continued. He glanced at her. All of the excitement he'd had when he pulled her up the steps was gone. She didn't know why.

"Mm-hmm," she murmured. She didn't want to talk about work.

He turned to her, something on his mind. "We agreed that we were going to be friends, right?" He swept his arm towards the dance floor and band, and the festivities beyond. "All of this is just...we're just...I mean, isn't that what we agreed?" He looked at her then looked away, as if the sight of her physically hurt him.

She nodded, "It is..."

Jamie's face fell and he gave her one last pained glance before dropping his gaze to the floor at their feet.

"Right," he said.

"But that's not what I want, Jamie," she said quietly.

His eyes shot up from the floor as if he could catch her words in the air if he was fast enough.

"What?" He didn't trust what he'd heard.

"That's not what I want. I don't want to be just friends with you."

There. She'd done it. She had told him the truth. Whatever the consequences, she could hold on to that much.

Jamie stared at her. He didn't speak or move or respond in any way. Just stared. Like she was an apparition that he couldn't believe was real.

Then, ever so slowly, a smile entered his eyes. It spread to the outer corners of his eyes so they crinkled. It lifted his cheeks, pulling up the corners of his mouth unevenly into his crooked grin. While joy moved across his face, his eyes held hers, filled with tenderness, disbelief, and longing. He pulled one of his gloves off and reached up to her face, barely touching her cheek with his fingers, cupping her chin in his hand.

"I was hoping you were going to say that." His crooked grin became his goofy smile and he lifted his gaze to the rafters, lightly tipping her head back so she would see.

Mistletoe.

Mistletoe everywhere.

Mistletoe madness.

Just like he'd told her he'd done years ago when he wanted to convince her to kiss him in the gazebo. Bunches of Mistletoe dangled along each of the eight rafters, over every inch of the ceiling, side-by-side with no space between them, all of it was covered with Mistletoe lit up by white Christmas lights.

She gasped with delight. Dazzled by the sight of it and the sentiment it held. When she looked back at Jamie he was watching her. His hand still brushing her cheek. When he spoke it was with the voice of a man returning home from a long journey. A patient man who had finally reached his destination.

"I love you, Abigail Ackerman. I have loved you for so, so long."

"Jamie," she said as she pressed his hand against her cheek, wanting him to touch her, wanting him to kiss her. "I love you, too."

In an instant he had his arm around her waist, pulling her to him as he bent towards her and touched his lips to hers. Carefully at first, as if she were made of porcelain and he didn't want to break her. Then he let his hand move from her cheek to her hair. He pushed his fingers into her curls and his kiss became firmer, more possessive.

Abigail didn't know she could lose herself so completely in a kiss. She had never known such a feeling could exist. As if she no longer needed the ground below her feet or air in her lungs. All she needed was Jamie.

As first kisses go, it was possibly one of the longest build ups ever known in Pitkin Point, seeing as they'd met when Abigail was in 3rd grade and Jamie was in 4th. But it made up for the long wait by being one of the most publicly romantic first kisses in the history of the town. One that nobody who knew them was surprised to see, but one that everyone was happy had finally come to be.

When Jamie pulled away from Abigail to tell her again, as he planned to for the rest of their lives, how much he loved her, a cheer erupted from the dance floor. Led by, among a handful of others, Zeke and Fern, who were two of the loudest voices. Surprised and suddenly shy from the attention, Abigail and Jamie ducked their heads in half bows to their impromptu audience.

The band played on and the couples returned to swirling across the floor under the starlit Christmas Eve night. Jamie turned back to Abigail, his eyes shining, and took her by the hand.

"Now we dance," he said.

And never was a truer statement ever spoken.

❄

THANK you for reading Mistletoe Madness! If you enjoyed this book you may enjoy the other books in the series...

Enchanting Eve - Halloween Romance

Love is at the Table - Thanksgiving Romance

New Year in Paradise - New Year's Eve Romance

❄

IF YOU'RE in the mood for another Christmas romance, get your copy of Charlotte's Christmas Charade the first book in A Sugar Plum Romance series – antics of chefs who get in over their heads at Christmas time and end up in charming holiday love stories!

Epilogue

Abigail looked anxiously out the front window of The Thinking Bean. The sky was overcast and cloudy and she hoped the weather reports were right. They had been calling for snow on Christmas Eve for the past week, and if she didn't get snow on her wedding day she was afraid she would be disappointed.

Snow was the perfect weather for her and Jamie to get married in, just as Christmas Eve was the perfect day. It had been one year to the day since they shared their first kiss in front of the whole town of Pitkin Point. And today they would share their first kiss as man and wife in the very same gazebo. Snow would make the day completely perfect.

"Abbah Dabbah, you look amazing!" Zeke said as he entered the cafe from the book section of the shop.

Her dress was pure white, off the shoulder with faux fur trim. Her bodice and long sleeves shimmered like ice in the light and had an extra dab of faux fur on her cuffs. The skirt flared out at just above her hips and fell elegantly to the floor in three layers with a short train trailing for just a few feet behind her when she walked. Abigail's hair was pulled up in an elaborate mass of dark, shining curls and decorated with red and white roses.

She turned to Zeke, who looked handsome himself in a black tuxedo complete with a Christmas red vest. He was Jamie's best man and had been fussing for weeks about his responsibilities. So far, he hadn't lost the rings or anything dramatic. However, they were all a little nervous about what he had planned for his best man toast at the reception.

"Don't let Jamie in here," Fern called to her fiancé. Zeke had popped the question to Fern over Thanksgiving. Abigail liked to think that her and Jamie's wedding plans had pushed her brother over the edge into finally proposing to Fern. She was Abigail's maid of honor and now her future sister-in-law. Abigail couldn't have wished for anyone whom she would rather call her best friend and her sister.

"I'm not letting him in anywhere," Zeke defended himself. "I'm just coming in to give my sister a good luck kiss before we head over to the gazebo. Everything ready?" Zeke was talking to Dillon who had followed him into the cafe area. He was Jamie's groomsmen, looking grown up and dapper in his tuxedo and green vest.

"Yup," Dillon grinned at Abigail. It was the same lopsided grin of his father's, and whenever she saw it Abigail's heart warmed. "Abby, you look beautiful," Dillon said, a fierce blush rushing up his cheeks. Still awkward and gangly like any 14-year old boy, but she found out every day what a wonderful young man he was.

"Thank you, Dillon," she reached out to him and he came to her to give her a hug. Zeke did as well, kissing her on the cheek.

"Okay, now out. Go manage the groom. He's loose if you two aren't with him," Fern shooed them on their way.

"These are ready," Judy informed them, holding up one of the bouquets she had been checking. She was Abigail's bridesmaid. Both Judy and Fern looked brilliant in their dresses. Judy in green, Fern in red. The bouquets, made up of pine, holly and red and white roses, contrasted beautifully with their dresses and the white of Abigail's.

Nothing much was left to do. Her parents, Fern, and Judy were to escort her across the street at the designated time and the wedding would commence. They had done some extra decorating at the gazebo by putting up a fresh Scotch Pine in the center. Decorating it with thousands of white lights as well as gold, red, green, and midnight blue ribbons and shining bulbs. Jamie's vest was midnight blue, in honor of her blue dress that had captured his heart so many years ago. And, of course, she wore a midnight blue ribbon in her hair as well as one hanging from her bouquet as her "something blue".

"It's almost time, sweetie," her Dad said.

Abigail glanced into the cloudy skies and looked for any sign of snowflakes. None yet. She sighed, then smiled. She knew Jamie was doing the same thing. They had both decided months ago that snow during their ceremony would be pretty epic. She knew he was keeping one eye on the clouds.

Besides the lack of snow, everything else about their ceremony, their life really, was pretty spot on perfect. At least for them it was perfect.

Abigail had been able to build a pretty decent freelance business over the past year, painting decorative windows for small businesses in Pitkin Point and surrounding towns. It was enjoyable work that paid well and left her a lot of free time, which she used to do some more traditional paintings on canvas. Just like she'd always dreamed of doing. Zeke had featured some of her artwork on the walls of the The Thinking Bean, and she'd even sold a few.

Jamie had found his calling when he got a job over the summer at the local plant nursery. He had quickly rose in the ranks to manager. Grace and Sam Jenkins, who owned the place, were looking at retiring in the next few years, and Jamie was considering buying the business from them and being his own boss. He loved the work and was very good at it. To Abigail, it seemed like an excellent fit for him.

"It's time," her Mom announced, beaming at her only daughter as she handed her the bridal bouquet. "You look gorgeous, sweetie."

"Thank you," Abigail said as she took her father's arm and the small wedding party walked across the street to the park.

They would be married at the gazebo, go to the town hall for a luncheon and cake, then join the Christmas Eve dance. The dance would act as the end of their reception. This way they could have what they both wanted, a small, intimate ceremony and celebration combined with a huge bash that allowed everyone in town to come.

As they drew closer to the gazebo, Abigail could see their friends and family sitting on the benches that had been set up facing the ceremony. The greenery on the gazebo had been bumped up a notch for their wedding. Add that to the tree glowing in the center, and the gazebo made an extraordinary backdrop for their vows.

Their favorite cellist, who now played regularly at The Thinking Bean, had agreed to perform for their wedding. The low notes of the cello floated in the air and made Abigail feel nothing less than regal. Jamie stood with the judge at the steps of the gazebo, looking tall and handsome, and maybe a little bit nervous. Her heart was beating with the excitement. Joy filled her whole body. The anticipation of seeing him, marrying him, and being his wife was almost too much to handle. But the ceremony was underway and she only had minutes to wait. She took a deep breath and soaked in the moment.

Her mother was escorted down the aisle by both Zeke

and Dillon, one on each arm. Then Fern walked down the aisle, smiling widely, taking her place right behind where Abigail would stand. Then Judy followed suit, standing behind Fern. Finally, it was Abigail and her father's turn.

All of the guests stood as the cellist played the wedding march. For the rest of her life, Abigail always remembered the feeling she had in that moment. It was just like the feeling she'd had when Jamie swept her off her feet on the dance floor. She felt like she was floating, like she was in a dream and Jamie was at the end of it, waiting for her, loving her.

The closer she got to him the wider he smiled and she thought that nothing could make her any happier than she was on that day. As he took her hand in his and they turned towards the judge to walk up the steps and be married in front of the Christmas tree, snow started to fall. The soft, sparkling snow that made up her dreams and, now, had made her dreams come true. Abigail looked into Jamie's laughing eyes and knew that she was blessed.

THE END

Also by Darci Balogh

More Sweet Holiday Romance Series (Box Set - great value!)

Want a quick escape over the holidays? These feel-good romances will get you in the spirit for Halloween, Thanksgiving, Christmas and a brand New Year!

1. Enchanting Eve
2. Love is at the Table
3. Mistletoe Madness (you've got it!)
4. New Year in Paradise

Dream Come True Series

1. Her Scottish Keep
2. Her British Bard
3. Her Sheltered Cove
4. Her Secret Heart
5. Her One and Only

Lady Billionaire Series

1. Ms. Money Bags
2. Ms. Perfect
3. Ms. Know-it-All

Sugar Plum Romance Series

Christmas, cooking, and chefs falling in love!

1. Charlotte's Christmas Charade
2. Bella's Christmas Blunder

Love & Marriage Contemporary Romance (Box Set - best bang for your buck!)

Steamy, emotional, relatable characters, these older woman, younger man romances are both racy and romantic.

1. The Quiet of Spring

2. For Love & For Money

3. Stars in the Sand

About the Author

Darci Balogh is a writer and indie filmmaker from Denver. She grew up in the beautiful mountains of Colorado and has lived in several areas of the state over her lifetime. She currently resides in Denver where she raised her two glorious, intelligent daughters to functioning adulthood. This is, by far, one of her highest achievements. She has a love-hate relationship with gardening, probably should dust more, adores dogs and is allergic to cats.

Darci has been a writer since she was a child and enjoys crafting stories into novels and screenplays. Big surprise, some of her favorite pastimes are reading and watching movies. Classic British TV is high on her 'Like' list, along with quietly depressing detective series and coffee with heavy cream.

Printed in Great Britain
by Amazon